FATHERLAND

By the same author

THE PARTY
COMEDIANS
ALL GOOD MEN *and* ABSOLUTE BEGINNERS
THROUGH THE NIGHT *and* SUCH IMPOSSIBILITIES
OCCUPATIONS
COUNTRY: A TORY STORY
OI FOR ENGLAND

Fatherland

TREVOR GRIFFITHS

faber and faber
LONDON · BOSTON

First published in 1987 by
Faber and Faber Limited
3 Queen Square London WC1N 3AU

Filmset by Wilmaset Birkenhead Wirral
Printed in Great Britain by
Redwood Burn Limited, Trowbridge, Wiltshire and
bound by Pegasus Bookbinding, Melksham, Wiltshire.

All rights reserved

© Trevor Griffiths 1987

Lines from 'Eldorado', lyrics © Wolff-Ekkehardt Stein and Wolfgang Jass,
are reproduced by kind permission of Autobahn Musikverlag and
Peer Musikverlag, Munich, Germany

Lines from 'Guilty', words and music by Randy Newman,
© 1973 Warner Bros Music and Randy Newman, are
reproduced by kind permission of Warner Bros Music Ltd.

*This book is sold subject to the condition that it shall not, by way of trade
or otherwise, be lent, resold, hired out or otherwise circulated without the
publisher's prior consent in any form of binding or cover other than that
in which it is published and without a similar condition including
this condition being imposed on the subsequent purchaser.*

British Library Cataloguing in Publication Data

Griffiths, Trevor, *1935–*
Fatherland.
I. Title
822'.914   PR6057.R52
ISBN 0–571–13659–1

Library of Congress Cataloging-in-Publication Data

Griffiths, Trevor.
Fatherland.
I. Title
PN1997.F3526 1986   791.43'72   8–11485
ISBN 0–571–13659–1 (pbk.)

Fatherland was first shown at the London Film Festival on the South Bank on 21 November 1986.

Cast:

KLAUS DRITTEMANN	Gerulf Pannach
EMMA	Fabienne Babe
LUCY	Cristine Rose
JAMES DRYDEN	Sigfrit Steiner
ROSA	Eva Krutina
MARITA	Heike Schrotter
SCHIFF	Hans Peter Hallwachs
UWE	Ronald Simoneit
CIA MAN	Marlowe Shute
JURGEN KIRSCH	Heinz Diesing
LAWYER/CLERK	Robert Dietl
THOMAS	Patrick Gillert
SENATOR HUNDHAMMER	Winfried Tromp
YOUNG DRITTEMANN	Thomas Oehlke
BRAUN	Jim Raketa
JOURNALIST	Bernard Bloch
MAX	Stephan Samuel

Director of Photography	Chris Menges
Editor	Jonathan Morris
Executive Producer	Irving Teitelbaum
Co-Producers	Fritz Buttenstedt and Marin Karmitz
Producer	Raymond Day
Director	Ken Loach

A Kestrel II film for Film Four International in association with Clasart Film and MK2.

Some work with the mind, some with the body.
Those who work with the mind rule others;
those who work with the body are ruled by others.
Those who are ruled carry others;
those who rule are carried by others.

Meng-Tse, *c.* 600 B.C.

Pretitle sequence

Black. A voice answers a question, press conference acoustic.
KLAUS DRITTEMANN: (*Out of shot, in German; objective*) . . . To be honest, I'm not here to talk about my country and its problems . . .
(*Colour. Slow scan of pads, pencils, reporters' dead faces sniffing the hiatus for a possible lead. A cough or two, a scrape of chair. Cameras click, wind on.*)
MALE JOURNALIST: (*Out of shot, German*) You're free to speak your mind, Herr Drittemann, here in the West . . . And criticism of the DDR's what your reputation's built on, isn't it? Seems odd you won't speak about it now.
(*Shot of* LUCY BERNSTEIN, *good suit, shoes, mid-thirties; quite tense, watchful in the silence. Shot of* WOLFGANG BRAUN, *lips pursed as he takes her look.*)
DRITTEMANN: (*Out of shot*) Let's say it doesn't interest me to speak about it.

Black and white. KLAUS DRITTEMANN, *jeans, shoulder-length hair, between two Stasi, back seat of Wartburg, being driven through dark East Berlin streets. The car stops outside an old apartment block. A young pregnant woman* (MARITA) *is pushed towards the car from an open doorway by two men and thrust into the front seat between driver and fourth Stasi. The journey resumes.*
DRITTEMANN *sees her in half-profile. She doesn't turn round. Sound of cell door clanging open.*
Black and white. DRITTEMANN *on haunches, back to whitewashed brick wall, prison clothes, short hair, stares up at the two State security police in the doorway.*
Black and white. DRITTEMANN *walks a pace ahead of the two police guards down the metallic corridor.*

LUCY BERNSTEIN: (*Over, American in German, press conference acoustic*) . . . I'm sure Herr Drittemann's happy to answer questions on any subject provided it's in the context of his work as an artist . . .

Black and white. A CLERK, *grizzled, early sixties, sits at a desk reading Drittemann's court file in the dim light of the table lamp.*
DRITTEMANN *stands in front of the desk. The two Stasi loom through the glazed glass of the door behind him.*
CLERK: So, young man. You're charged with actions hostile to socialism and in breach of the constitution. How will you plead?
DRITTEMANN: I don't plead.
CLERK: Mmm. You deny this is your work, for instance?
(*He's spread a fly-sheet on the desk: 'DEFEND RED PRAGUE'.*)
DRITTEMANN: No.
CLERK: Then you must plead guilty.
DRITTEMANN: Then I don't need a trial.
CLERK: You don't help yourself. You have some problems, young man.
DRITTEMANN: The problem's yours, not mine.
CLERK: Stalinism, oh yes. (*Stands. Thinks. Reopens the file.*) I suppose the son of Jacob Drittemann would have to say the problem was ours . . . mmm?
(DRITTEMANN *says nothing, his contempt palpable. A German shepherd dog barks in the courtyard below. The* CLERK *crosses to a window, peels a curtain, reveals the distant electric powerhouse of West Berlin against the sky. When he speaks again, the voice has turned to metal.*)
Stalinism. Tearing a piece from that filthy shit world over there and trying to make it decent. With 70 per cent of your population born and raised under Fascism. Against a world whose whole logic is to stop us from succeeding. So that for every deutschmark you spend building the new world, you have to spend another defending it. We pay the price. Because this way, in time, the flowers will one day bloom. (*Turns, looks at* DRITTEMANN.) We didn't spend our years in camps and gaols under Fascism to hand back what we'd fought for to the same old bitch who'd made this shit world

in the first place. If that's Stalinism . . .
(*He shrugs, returns slowly to his chair.* DRITTEMANN *says nothing. The Stasi stir in the corridor outside.*)
Two, two and a half years. Less if you plead guilty, mercy of the court and so on. (*He leaves space for a reply he doesn't really expect.*) All right.
(*He presses a button below the desk, the door opens, a guard fills the doorway.*)
Wait.
(*Waves the guard out again.*)
You may be beyond advice, particularly from the likes of me, but I'll say it anyway. I did ten years. It's important not to let it break you. (*Pause.*) I found it helped to spell out every day *why* I was there. (*Pause.*) Hold on to what you value. In the end, it's all you have.
(*Button again. Guards appear. The old* CLERK *nods.*)
DRITTEMANN: Thanks.

Black and white. Corridor. DRITTEMANN *leads the guards back to the cell. Opening piano chords of Drittemann's 'In Praise of Nicaragua', press conference exchanges continuing over.*
JOURNALIST: (*Voice over, English,* Time Out) Any words for the people you left behind, Mr Drittemann?
DRITTEMANN: (*Voice over, in English*) Yes. 'It's all the same fuckin' day, man.' Janis Joplin.
JOURNALIST: (*Voice over, with it*) Right!
(*The figures have dwindled, left the frame. The corridor stills. Music up and:*)

Titles:

Black and white still sequence essentializing Klaus Drittemann's life from gaol to now: release, head shaved; search for work; waiter in café; building-site labourer; electrician at transformer factory; marriage to Marita; the child Thomas; estrangement, separation; learning guitar, hair long again; youth club gigs, church hall, bars; surveillance; harassment.
Over, Drittemann's 'Nicaragua' song, Sprechstimme parts by Drittemann alone, sung by friends at the farewell party. (First scene.)

Black and white. Interior. Marita's apartment, Nuschkestrasse, East Berlin. Night.
Caption: *Actually Existing Socialism.*
Off, at the piano, DRITTEMANN *and friends approach the song's end. Track establishes nineteenth-century apartment, large, dilapidated, draughty, book-lined, filled with people drinking, singing, talking, dancing across two rooms and a corridor.* MARITA *stands in a listening group with her second husband,* HANS PETER. *Song ends, to applause. People press* DRITTEMANN *for more. He shakes his head, carries his red wine towards the rear of the apartment, stopping en route to hug* MARITA *and* HANS PETER.
In German:
DRITTEMANN: I have to speak with Thomas.
MARITA: (*Kissing his cheek*) Take him some cake.
    (*Vissotsky ambles into 'Troy' on the adjoining room's hi-fi, to cheers and da-da accompaniment.* DRITTEMANN *makes his way to the kitchen, cuts a slice of the long flat chocolate cake Marita's made, already down to '. . . Wiedersehen Dritt . . .' A young man, nineteen, East Berlin sharp, puts his head round the door.*)
MAX: Time you leave tomorrow?
DRITTEMANN: Ten-ish. Why?
MAX: Got a job on, need your guardian angels out of the way early. Couldn't make it nine, could you, comrade?
DRITTEMANN: (*Leaving, plate in hand*) Maybe. Got to see my kid, OK?

Black and white. Interior. Bedroom, tiny, dark; dim street light through uncurtained window. THOMAS, *fourteen, eyes open, lies on his side in the bed. A knock. The eyes close. The door opens.*
DRITTEMANN: (*Soft*) Tom. You awake? (*Closes door behind him, approaches bed.*) Tom.
    (*The kid opens his eyes, pulls away slightly as* DRITTEMANN *sits on the bed.*)
    Want some cake?
THOMAS: No thanks.
    (*Silence.* DRITTEMANN *lays it down on the wood floor.*)
DRITTEMANN: You gonna be OK?

THOMAS: Yes.

DRITTEMANN: I'm not going because I want to, Tom. You understand that?

THOMAS: Yes.

DRITTEMANN: They won't let me work here.
  (*Nothing.*)
  I'll call, I'll write, I'll send money. And as soon as they let me have a visa to, I'll be back.

THOMAS: Fine.
  (*The boy's passivity hurts.* DRITTEMANN *looks for words; can't find them.*)

DRITTEMANN: OK. Work hard. Do what you have to.
  (*He kisses the boy's brow. The boy takes his hand, holds it for a moment, releases it.* DRITTEMANN *moves towards the door.*)

THOMAS: Go well, Dad.
DRITTEMANN: (*Doorway; grateful*) You too, kid.
(*The boy turns on his side.* DRITTEMANN *closes the door, moves back to the party, passing* MAX *and others by the hall doorway.*)
MAX: Klaus. This is for you. (*Gives him an old black leather overcoat.*) Keep you warm in the West.
DRITTEMANN: (*Grinning*) I'll look like the bloody Stasi. Thanks.
MAX: So. Nine o'clock tomorrow. What do you say?
DRITTEMANN: What's the deal anyway?
MAX: Old leather gear, fetching a bomb over there, I've cornered the market, fifty marks for this piece of shit, (*Touches the coat he's just given* DRITTEMANN) in the hand, this guy's getting four hundred for 'em . . .
DRITTEMANN: (*En route*) And you think *you've* cornered the market? The bulls're gonna take your balls away sooner or later, comrade . . .
MAX: That'll be the day. Ha!
(*The tape on the hi-fi slides into Sniff 'n' the Tears: 'Eldorado'.* MARITA *takes* DRITTEMANN's *hand, draws him into the room where people dance or sit, drink, talk and watch, and begins to dance with him.*)
MARITA: How was he?
DRITTEMANN: Tough.
MARITA: He'll be fine.
DRITTEMANN: I think he thinks I *want* to go.
MARITA: No he doesn't. Sh.
(*They dance. Draw closer. He strokes her hair, touches her temple with his lips. Their dance grows heavy, scarcely moving. On the tape, Sniff has:*)
> Seen trumpetin' herds
> Fine feathered birds
> Blacken up the sky;
> Pick at the bones
> Of the man who left home
> To search for gold and die.
> Saw Cortés conquer Mexico

*Pissaro take Peru,
I'd give all the gold in Eldorado
Just to be with you.*

Black and white. Interior. 2.30 a.m. HANS PETER, MARITA *and* DRITTEMANN *play Skat for pfennigs in the kitchen area. There's a low-tone discussion of the Polish question under way in the next room: it's serious, wide-ranging, well-informed; men more than women, but not exclusively; the thrust and tenor of argument are socialist rather than 'dissident', anti-party not anti-DDR.*
The three play Skat with habituated, casual speed. MARITA *and* DRITTEMANN *share a joke; she kisses his cheek; she wins a difficult contract; it's a close count,* DRITTEMANN *was sure she'd lose.* DRITTEMANN *shells out.* HANS PETER *watches, likes them both.*
HANS PETER: (*Paying up*) That's me. I'm on earlies, crack of dawn. I wish you well, comrade. (*They shake hands across the table.*) We'll miss you. (*He kisses* MARITA's *hair.*) I'll get Thomas off to school, if you like . . .
(MARITA *squeezes his hand, nods her thanks. He leaves for his bed.*)
MARITA: I'll get some things.
(*She wanders off to the bathroom through the débris.*
DRITTEMANN *moves to the connecting doorway, studies the talking group from the shadows, his people. Eventually he's noticed, invited to join in, says he has to go. Handshakes, hugs, advice gently given, cheeks gently kissed. There's a reference to his father in the West and to how much he's missed in the DDR.*
MARITA's *reappeared, stands watching him from the hall, wash-bag in hand. He crosses to join her. By the time they reach the front door the Polish question has been resumed, Adam Schaff and Kolakowski the basic ground of argument.*)

Black and white. Interior. DRITTEMANN's *apartment, one large room lit faintly by street light. The floors are piled with tea chests, boxes, packing-cases.* DRITTEMANN *lies on the floor-mattress, half-propped, naked, watching* MARITA *insert her cap at the foot of the bed. Over, fragments of the West Berlin press conference.*

They make love, direct, honest, unsentimental, pleasures voiced openly in the empty room, sliding and dipping in folds of custom and trust. The conference voices probe on.

Black and white. Interior. Later. They lie near sleep.
DRITTEMANN: Can you remember why we ever split up?
MARITA: (*After thought*) Oh yes.
   (*They laugh. Phone rings, bridging to:*)

Interior. Morning. Drittemann's room. DRITTEMANN *at window, phone in hand, staring down on the street. He listens to his caller, watches the grey Wartburg parked opposite and the two men in the front seat.*
DRITTEMANN: (*Eventually*) . . . That's fine. No, that's good. I'm most grateful . . . Give me the name again. (*He writes it down.*) She speaks German? OK, I'll watch out for her, thanks for calling.
   (*He puts the receiver down, studies the name on the pad, tears the page out, puts it in his pocket, writes something else on the pad, carries it to the mattress, where* MARITA *sleeps, lays it by her pillow. Collects grip and guitar, lays them by the door, returns to the window, watches the men in the Wartburg. Bring up their conversation. Cut to:*)

Black and white. Exterior. Street. Car interior. The DRIVER's *finishing his joke. His colleague listens, watching the steps and doorway to Drittemann's apartment block over the other* MAN's *shoulder.*
DRIVER: . . . So the police follow him, right, a few miles, wave him down, there's a whole family of them in the car, they tell him he's won a Good Driving Award, 300 marks, right? And the guy says, (*drunk's voice*) 'God be thanked, I thought you wanted to see my licence, I haven't passed my driving test yet' . . . And his wife leans over and says, 'Take no notice, officer, he'll say anything when he's pissed' . . . And the kid in the back seat says, 'I told you no good'd come of driving a stolen car, Dad' . . . And then the boot flies open and out pops old grannie and shouts, 'Are we

in the West yet?'
(*The* SECOND MAN *grunts, a mirthless rictus passing for laughter.* DRITTEMANN *has appeared in the doorway at the top of the steps; guitar, grip, jeans, plimsolls.*)
SECOND MAN: Here's the little fruit-cake.
(DRITTEMANN *looks carefully up and down the street for some moments. The* DRIVER *contacts a second car by radio.*)
Watch out.
(DRITTEMANN'S *heading straight for the car. The* DRIVER *closes his radio compartment. The two men stare fixedly through the windscreen as* DRITTEMANN'S *head appears in the driver's rolled-down window.*)
DRITTEMANN: Good day. I wonder if I might trouble one of you gentlemen for a light?
(*The* DRIVER *fiddles in his pocket, the* SECOND MAN *hands his cigarette across.*)
' Most kind. (*Casual, lighting up*) If it's of any help, I'll be at the Karl Liebknecht Transformer Factory visiting my stepfather until ten, at my mother's house in Friedrichshagen thereafter – you have the address, I believe – a quick visit to the Visa Office and away. (*Sweet smile, handing cigarette back*) It's been a pleasure being followed by you, gentlemen . . .
DRIVER: You're gonna trip over your hair, creambun.
(DRITTEMANN *smiles, leaves. The* SECOND MAN *gets out to follow. The* DRIVER *turns the car round, radioing ahead. On the pavement,* DRITTEMANN *passes* MAX *and his West Berlin dealer, blond crewcut, around forty.* MAX *winks as they pass.* DRITTEMANN *walks towards camera. Back of shot,* MAX *and the* DEALER *pass the walking Stasi, then the Wartburg three-point-turning in the narrow street.*
DRITTEMANN *reaches the S-Bahn stairway on the corner, jumps suddenly in the air, rams the imagined perfect cross into the back of the net and disappears down the steps.*)

Black and white. Interior. Medium close up of Drittemann's note to Marita on the pillow, a lock of her hair in shot. It reads, in English:
'Here's looking at you. K.'

Bring up factory sounds and cut to:

Interior. Karl Liebknecht Transformer Factory. DRITTEMANN's *point of view, through passageway window, of a large work-bay. The night shift of eight men and a woman sit in silence in a rough half-circle around two factory security police and the shift leader,* JURGEN KIRSCH, *late fifties, Drittemann's stepfather. Cigarettes are smoked and butted down the long silence.*
DRITTEMANN *scans the bay; checks an official notice posted on a new Swedish computerized process: 'This machine already does the work of forty people.' Underneath, sprayed, a neat job, 'I bet it never does the Central Committee out of a job though.'*
The Stasi stand eventually, the period for voluntary admissions over, point to the graffiti, mutter to KIRSCH *and leave. The tired group rise, stretch, cough, begin to clear up and depart for their beds.*
KIRSCH *notices* DRITTEMANN *through the window, waves to the tiny office at the top of the iron ladder. Workers pass* DRITTEMANN *on his way through; he's known here, an ex-colleague; there are smiles, winks, greetings.*

Black and white. Interior. Office. KIRSCH, *big, beefy, changes to day clothes.* DRITTEMANN *in doorway.*
KIRSCH: Have you seen your mother yet?
DRITTEMANN: Not yet, no . . .
KIRSCH: What time you leaving?
DRITTEMANN: There's time. OK?
    (*A young* KID, *twenty maybe, arrives in the doorway, East Berlin version of skinhead, copper stud in left ear.*)
KID: Wanna see me, Chief?
    (KIRSCH *shouts 'Bastard', dives for the wastepaper basket, takes out a spraycan and hurls it at the lad in the door.*)
KIRSCH: You do anything like that again, bollock brain, and I'll drive my boot so far up your arse people'll think we're a married couple . . .
KID: Sorry, Chief, couldn't resist it . . .
KIRSCH: Piss off.
    (*The* KID *scarpers.* KIRSCH *changes his party badge from overalls to jacket-lapel. Winks grimly at* DRITTEMANN.)

He's worse than you were, that bugger. I need a beer.

Black and white. Exterior. Factory yards, kilometres of them.
KIRSCH *and* DRITTEMANN *head for the gates in extreme long shot; conversation over.*
DRITTEMANN: Why didn't you shop him? Two years to pension, if they'd found the spraycan in your wastebin . . .
KIRSCH: I'll tell you why, songmaker, it's because he's the only one on the shift can make the bloody thing *work*, that's why . . . We've got a contract for Africa to meet and behind bars he's good for nothing, are you kidding, I know my socialist duty, comrade . . . And don't you go forgetting yours in the West, OK? Mind the train . . .
(*They stop, tiny in the vastness, to let the engine pass.* KIRSCH *rasps on, fierce, Friesian here and there.*)
. . . You're so bloody *innocent* man. God knows what *they'll* do with you over there . . .
DRITTEMANN: (*Laughing, fond*) Bollocks.
KIRSCH: Bollocks, he says. Ha.

Black and white. Exterior. Factory gates, industrial street. They show IDs to the security police, pass through. KIRSCH *stops at the top of the stairs to the S-Bahn.*
KIRSCH: Listen, I'll leave you here, that paint nonsense has put me behind, I've some union things to sort out . . .
DRITTEMANN: I thought you were coming back . . .
KIRSCH: Yes, well . . . Better you see her alone . . . (*He looks away, looks back.*) I'm sorry you're going. I wish there were some other way . . .
(*They shake hands, wordless; hug.*)
DRITTEMANN: Listen. Thanks.
(*They detach. It's a hard parting.*)
KIRSCH: Don't forget us, eh?
(*He waves his hand at the DDR around him.* DRITTEMANN *shakes his head, grave, still.*)
Shall I call Rosa, say you're on your way . . . ?
DRITTEMANN: (*Smiling*) I *will* go, it's all right . . .
KIRSCH: Good. (*Pause.*) I saw a funny thing last night.

DRITTEMANN: What was that?
KIRSCH: I saw your mother weep. (*Looks at the sky. Straightens his Willy Brandt cap.*) It's gonna rain.
(*He smiles, ambles away down the road.* DRITTEMANN *watches him for a while, as the sound drains.*)
JOURNALIST: (*American, voice over*) Could you say what it is you value most about being in the West, Mr Dritteburg?
DRITTEMANN: (*Deadpan*) Anonymity.

Black and white. Interior. Close up of framed family pic of the Drittemanns, early 1950s. Jacob sits importantly at his desk, the chair swivelled to face camera, the children (Mechtild, seven; Klaus, six), in Young Pioneer neckerchief, at his knees. Rosa stands, suit and shoes, a fraction detached. Over this, the sounds of an English lesson, ROSA *and a* YOUNG BOY, *in the adjoining room: she's teaching the structure 'It is'.*
DRITTEMANN *scans the room that was his father's: books, paintings, Heartfield prints, old darkwood furniture, carpet over wood floor; a place of hard comfort. Through the window, the green suburb of Friedrichshagen, quarter for artists and professionals for generations, flanking the long grey span of the Muggelsee.*
A partition opens behind him, he turns, sees his mother. She looks at him steadily for some moments, then closes the partition behind her with precise hands, crosses to the desk, lights a cigarette like one who could do it in her sleep.
ROSA: (*Matter-of-fact*) Sit down, won't you.
DRITTEMANN: (*Defensive*) How long have you got?
ROSA: Long enough. Sit down.
(*He takes an armchair. She sits at the desk, chair angled to face him.*)
Did you say goodbye to your stepfather?
DRITTEMANN: Yes.
(*The* BOY *rehearses a structure beyond the partition: 'It is cold, it is not cold.'*)
ROSA: You will be missed here. But it's your own choice.
DRITTEMANN: If you say so.
ROSA: What would you say?
DRITTEMANN: I've had the bum's rush, they've shown me the

door, something like that . . . I think the choice-factor's been pretty minimal . . .
ROSA: (*Sharp*) No one says you must go . . .
DRITTEMANN: (*Hard*) *Logic* says I must go . . .
ROSA: (*Through him*) . . . You put personal problems before the struggles of the people . . .
DRITTEMANN: . . . They've stopped me from ad*dress*ing the struggles of the people . . .
ROSA: . . . Don't be so innocent. You left them no choice.
(*The wheel stops where it began. Ironies hover in the still room, but* DRITTEMANN *has the taste not to invoke them. Next door, the* BOY's *English grows more Prussian: 'It is true, it is not true; it is untrue, it is not untrue.'*)
I spoke with Comrade Steppat earlier, he's ringing back, he says the decision not to grant you a return-visa was a close-run thing . . .
DRITTEMANN: (*Leaning back, eyes heavy*) Mother . . .
ROSA: You have admirers on that Committee; behave responsibly, in six months, maybe a year, Steppat says, you could have your licence back and be performing again . . . This country made you, Klaus. Bore you, taught you, fed you, clothed you, gave you skills. These are your people. Leave and you spit in their faces.
(*They sit a moment, locked in an ancient argument, cuffed to their particular history of abrasion and conflict.*)
DRITTEMANN: Mother, I don't want this discussion.
ROSA: Perhaps not. But life is rarely a question of what we *want*, Klaus.
(DRITTEMANN *gets up, crosses to the window, struggles for a control he's not sure he can summon, stares at the matt grey of the Muggelsee under rain, the grey Wartburg parked across the street.*)
DRITTEMANN: Socialism has to live in people, individuals – you, me, Steppat, Honnecker, Gorbachev – or it lives nowhere. Not Proudhon. Not Bakunin . . . Not some petit-bourgeois individualist with idealist-subjectivist tendencies. Marx: *Grundrisse*. I want socialism. My wanting it is part of the socialism I want. I claim importance not for

myself but for what I do. When I no longer do it honestly, stop trying to speak the truth, keep my head down, behave more 'responsibly', concentrate on my career, give the statutory four security police at every gig I do, material so impeccably correct, so perfectly official that even *their* diseased sensibilities cannot fault it – that's when I'll be spitting on the people, Mother. And they will let me know it. (*Pause.*) If these are my people, who has the right to deny me their company? (*Faces her at last.*) Tell Steppat from me, the son of Jacob Drittemann cannot sing on his knees; and if he's to be silent, he'd sooner be silent where it matters less.

(*The phone has begun ringing in the adjoining room.* ROSA *stands, detaching from his bleak gaze, draws the partition back a precise body's width, crosses to answer it.* DRITTEMANN *begins to gather his things, worn by the encounter. He can see her head, swathed in smoke, through the opening; aches for warmth, contact, chilled by their habitual factuality.*
The young pioneer appears in the opening. Stares at DRITTEMANN. *Withdraws.* ROSA *addresses the boy briefly, returning; draws the partition closed again behind her; lights up another cigarette.*)

ROSA: That was Steppat. Wanted to speak to you. I told him you'd already left.

DRITTEMANN: I'll go . . .

ROSA: (*Abrupt*) Are you in touch with your father?

DRITTEMANN: (*Terse*) Not at all.

ROSA: But you'll look for him, am I right?

DRITTEMANN: I might.

(*She opens a drawer in the bureau, reaches deep inside for something, comes out with a key and ticket tied together by a piece of string. She hands them to him. He studies them frowningly.*)

ROSA: There were things he left behind, your hero-father, when he fled the country. I thought it safer to keep them in the West. They're yours now . . . Perhaps they'll help you . . . understand him a little better . . .

DRITTEMANN: I don't understand . . .

ROSA: It doesn't matter. One day you will. Go please. I have a child waiting.
(DRITTEMANN *gathers his things; hovers, going, staying.*
ROSA *sits wanly, not looking.*)
DRITTEMANN: Any message? If I find him?
(*She shakes her head.*)
What about my sister?
(*A beat. Another shake of the head. He nods, leaves. She watches him through the window down the path to the road. The grey Wartburg slides slowly into motion in his wake. Bring up S-Bahn sounds and cut to:*)

Black and white. Interior. S-Bahn, green country. Afternoon now.
DRITTEMANN *sits in largely empty compartment, staring unyieldingly at his tail some bays away, who stares coldly back at him. Between them, by the door, three hard-looking West Berlin tramps on a cheap day's piss-up in the East stand weaving and glugging, bottles of Schnapps and Falkener (DDR whisky) glinting in their blackened hands. Fragments of their chat drift about the dead space: their theme is freedom.*

Black and white. Exterior. Sequence of images of DRITTEMANN *saying goodbye to his city in the late afternoon: Alexanderplatz, Karl Marx Allee, Griefswald . . . Song: 'Hare in the Gate'.*

Interior. Border control point. Close shot of computer VDU, as Klaus Drittemann's state biography unfolds: a longish story.
DRITTEMANN's *face, watching through glass.* GUARD's *face, eyes down. Lifetimes elapse, stars die, in the silence. Shot of passport, open; visa; the* GUARD's *hand, a white finger scratching arhythmically on the edge of the book.*
DRITTEMANN *waits, a bunch of daffodils in his arms. The* GUARD's *hand flicks without warning, the passport lands neatly on the counter above, a practised effect.* DRITTEMANN *leaves it, waiting for the eyes. The* GUARD, *all of twenty, continues to scan the screen impassively. Looks up at last, ice in glass. Nods.*

Black and white. Exterior. Dusk. DRITTEMANN *emerges from*

brick and concrete complex on to deserted street. Behind him, the DDR control point and road barrier. Ahead in the murk, the West Berlin barrier. Beyond that, in the further distance, the light on a police car flashes in silent whirls. Sound comes and goes, unreal. After some moments, as he begins his walk to the West, the whirling light registers blue.

As DRITTEMANN enters the Western sector the film moves into full colour.

Interior. Close shot of computer VDU unfolding Drittemann's Western profile: a longish story using much the same data as before. DRITTEMANN waits, flowers below the face, framed through glass. Receives the nod.

Interior. Reception area, border control complex, West Berlin; mainly glass and lights, bright with artificial colours, heaving with sound-killing carpet.

Caption: *Great Freedom Street (Grossefreiheitstrasse).*
DRITTEMANN *emerges from control. A* WOMAN *approaches. She's around forty, tall, strong-bodied, dressed for success. She speaks rough but serviceable German with an American accent.*
WOMAN: *(Out of shot)* Herr Drittemann?
DRITTEMANN: That's right.
WOMAN: Lucy Bernstein, Taube Records. Welcome.
   (*They shake hands. She looks at the flowers. He remembers why he bought them, hands them to her. A flash-camera whirrs, clicks, close by.* DRITTEMANN'*s eyes sharpen.*)
It's all right, Uwe's with the firm, it's for the launch. Thank you. They're lovely. Come, I have a car . . .

Interior. Basement car park, border control complex. Lift doors open, they enter the tastefully lit space. The photographer, UWE, *says goodnight, heads for his Golf.* LUCY *leads* DRITTEMANN *through the sprinkle of cars towards her Mercedes 190E. Ahead, seen in Drittemann's point of view, two men sit smoking in an unlit Audi.*

DRITTEMANN *follows the woman past it, then on impulse returns, ducks down to ask the men for a light. A lit cigarette's passed to him,* DRITTEMANN *lights his Marlboro, hands it back with a thank-you smile. Between the two men, Drittemann's point of view, a car telephone.*
He strides out, catches up with LUCY *as she approaches her car.*
DRITTEMANN: (*Seeing it*) Aha.

Exterior. Basement car park interface with street. The Mercedes 190E approaches the barrier. Behind it, at a distance, the Audi follows. When the first car arrives at the barrier we see it's DRITTEMANN *driving.* LUCY *reaches across him to pay the ticket.*
DRITTEMANN: (*Voice over*) Do you gamble?
LUCY: (*Voice over*) No. How do you mean?
DRITTEMANN: Left or right, here?
LUCY: Left . . .
DRITTEMANN: I say the car behind's going right.
LUCY: It must be even money.
DRITTEMANN: No. It's a certainty.
   (*The barrier's raised, the Merc purrs forwards, swings a slow right. The Audi follows.*)

Interior. Mercedes at high speed on autobahn. DRITTEMANN *checks the mirror several times; catches the woman's bemused glance; smiles.*
DRITTEMANN: Where now?
LUCY: Next right and pull over. I'd like to get you home in one piece.
   (*Shot of car leaving motorway and pulling over. Over this:*)
   In the West we have a word for this, you know.
DRITTEMANN: Yes?
LUCY: Paranoia.
DRITTEMANN: We call it by its proper name where I come from.
LUCY: What's that?
DRITTEMANN: Surveillance.

Montage of shots of the car's traverse of the city, taking in a fair part of the six kilometres of Kurfürstendamm at night. Interlaced, car

interiors: LUCY *driving,* DRITTEMANN *scanning the hyperactive terrain of a West Berlin evening: punks, drunks, GIs, Turkish guest-workers, whores, hurrahs, leatherboys, street-clowns, neon, food, peep shows, police cars, design, display. A First World showroom, facing East. Street sounds and fragments of dialogue, asynchronous, displaced, and Joe Cocker's 'Fun Time' bind the sequence.*
Bedded in, lip-synched, the following scene:
The 190E draws up at traffic signals. A peep show lights pavement and car interior.
DRITTEMANN: What is it?
LUCY: Peep show? It's a place where men pay to see parts from women's bodies.
DRITTEMANN: (*Eventually*) Of.
LUCY: What?
DRITTEMANN: *Of* women's bodies.
LUCY: Oh. Is my German bad then?
DRITTEMANN: (*In English*) No worse than my English, I think.
LUCY: (*In English*) Ah. This is a bonus.
   (*A drunk stares at them from the lurid pavement; waves as they draw away from him. From here onwards, they speak with each other in English.*)

Interior. First floor apartment, Droysenstrasse, off Ku'damm.
DRITTEMANN *walks the four connecting rooms, takes in the sparse taste of the furnishings, returns eventually to the vast principal room, where Joe Cocker has eight bars of 'Fun Time' left on the hi-fi and* LUCY BERNSTEIN *conducts a terse exchange with New York on the telephone.* DRITTEMANN *walks round the small mound of his previously forwarded belongings, approaches the long black perspex table, studies once again the materials spread across it. He picks up a thickish contract, flicks pages, puts it down, passes on to a printed party invitation (Rainer Schiff and Taube Records invite you to meet Klaus Drittemann . . .), a small heap of fan mail, several bank statements, an alternative newspaper in Dutch, details of the forthcoming press conference, and half-a-dozen mock-ups of record covers, all featuring Drittemann. He gives the mock-ups careful, impassive attention, as Cocker 'Watches the River Flow': sees*

himself in evening dress at a banquet, surrounded by the rich and the beautiful; arriving at a mythic border control, guitar on his back, under the title Grossefreiheitstrasse; in combat uniform of the Sandinista.
LUCY's *call ends. She joins him at the table.*
LUCY: (*Over mock-ups, carrying on from where the call interrupted*) These are just ideas. We'd like your views . . . This is fan mail since 'In Praise of Nicaragua' was released. Did you get through the contract?
DRITTEMANN: I looked.
LUCY: (*Businesslike*) The Chief here's quite keen to announce the signing at the press conference, if that's at all possible . . .
(*She waits. He says nothing.*)
The apartment's all right?
(*He nods.*)
I still have bits and pieces here, which I'll move as and when. Bank statements . . . You've about twenty thousand dollars worldwide in royalties, but I don't imagine money's going to be a problem, once Taube has you on its books and the tour's been agreed. What else? A few lunches and dinner dates around town; the welcome party . . . Do you know Rainer Schiff? He's agreed to hold it at his place . . .
DRITTEMANN: Never met him.
LUCY: He's been pretty successful since he came West.
DRITTEMANN: So I heard.
LUCY: (*Checking table items again*) . . . The press conference . . . and that's about it. What do you want to do about food? I could book a table somewhere. Or there's stuff in the fridge if you'd sooner put your feet up . . .
(*She leaves the question hanging, begins to gather the mock-ups into their portfolio.* DRITTEMANN *crosses to the hi-fi, where Cocker's confessing 'It's Hard to Say, the Writing's on the Wall', clicks it off. She looks at him across the room.*)
DRITTEMANN: What happened to Taube?
(*She doesn't understand.*)
Herr Taube.
LUCY: Taube? We bought him out two years ago. You didn't know?

DRITTEMANN: Who's we?
LUCY: A & N. American and National, that was head office, New York, on . . . (*She's reckoning how much he has not understood.*) Jesus, have I goofed, I'd better start again . . .
DRITTEMANN: No no, not necessary, I've understood. It wasn't clear how it applied to myself. (*Pause.*) Now it is.
(*Silence. She probes meanings. He offers none.*)
LUCY: Taube's still Taube, nothing's changed here on the ground, Wolfgang Braun's in charge, do you know him . . . ?
DRITTEMANN: I know only Taube.
(*A pause. Hard to fill.*)
LUCY: The point is: the people here think you're an important talent and American and National are prepared to back their judgement. (*She points at the swill of things on the table.*) That's how all this applies to you. (*She collects her scarf, gloves, pigskin document case from a table.*) I've left my number by the phone there, if you need anything I'll be in most of the evening. (*She's by the arch to the hallway.*) Everyone's free to be proud, Mr Drittemann. I'm not sure any of us has the right to be stupid. Goodnight.
(*She leaves. He follows, surprised at the taut speed.*)
DRITTEMANN: Miss Bernstein . . .
(*She turns in the hall doorway.*)
. . . Did you succeed in finding my father?
LUCY: I'm afraid not. (*Beat.*) But we've managed to locate a Dutch journalist who might be of help . . . I've left something by her on the table . . .
DRITTEMANN: Thank you.
(*They look at each other steadily for some moments. She smiles, a little wryness in the eyes.*)
LUCY: They said you might be difficult.
DRITTEMANN: (*Simple*) I?
LUCY: The contract's important. The rest's pretty well up to you.
(*She leaves. He considers her meanings, turns back into the main room, picks up his long Scotch, gathers the phone, carries it towards the bathroom, dialling as he goes. Begins to piss at*

the lavatory, waiting for an answer.)
DRITTEMANN: (*German; to phone*) Hans Peter? Klaus. OK. So so. Is Marita there? Ahunh. And Thomas is with her? Ahunh. Yes, it's (*checks*) . . . 231876 . . . Fine. Thanks, comrade.
(*Puts receiver down, zips up. Gazes round the elegant chamber. Runs the back of his fingers along several items of silk underwear, cream and brown, hanging from a shower rail. Returns to the main room and the table. Takes it thoughtfully in again. Ends on the Dutch article. The word 'Nazi' figures in the headline. There's a by-line pic of the author: Emma de Baen; and a murky full-length photograph of a man leaning against a canal lock gate.*)

(*Wall Dream*); *black and white; mute. Point of view of a flight through undercity sewers. Close shot* KLAUS DRITTEMANN, *fleeing. Sounds invade the muteness, distorted barks, cries, fade abruptly.* DRITTEMANN *reaches cul-de-sac; stares upwards; sees hazardous iron steps lead up to a distant sky. He climbs, grim; on and on. Faint sounds of classical piano as he approaches the top. Arrives. Drags himself on to the parapet of a great wall, feels his face drenched in a glow of gold, sees* JACOB DRITTEMANN (*early 1950s*) *in evening dress seated at a Bechstein beckoning him to look at the glow's source, a key and a ticket in his hand.* DRITTEMANN *stands, turns, stares. In his point of view, he sees himself and the wall he stands on reflected in a huge mirror, but his father and the piano have gone. As he stares, the words 'Long Live Actually Existing Capitalism' are sprayed in red over the mirror's surface.*

Interior. A key fits into a box-lock, turns, is withdrawn.
MAN: (*Voice over, German*) I'll be outside.
(*Footsteps recede. A second key is inserted; turned. A second hand joins the first, to lift the lid.* DRITTEMANN's *point of view of the box contents: an oilskin package perhaps two feet square, a note pinned neatly to it. The hands open the note.*)
ROSA: (*Voice over*) To whom it may concern. I, Rosa Drittemann, certify that the enclosed items are the property of my ex-husband Jacob Drittemann. Signed, Rosa

Drittemann, 6th day of October, 1953.
(DRITTEMANN *lays the oilskin package on the table; touches it; would like to open it; can't or won't. He's had his hair cut, prison style, almost to the scalp.*)

Exterior. Zoo. Primates touch and tease their ritual way to pleasure. DRITTEMANN *watches, one of a crowd. The agency photographer takes pictures,* LUCY BERNSTEIN *by his side.*

Exterior. Zoo. Terrace café. DRITTEMANN *sits with a coffee and a Marlboro, the oilskin package on the table before him. In his point of view, some way away,* LUCY BERNSTEIN *waits to greet a man getting out of a taxi. At the next table, the agency photographer,* UWE, *rigs his tripod with dependable discretion.* DRITTEMANN *reads Rosa's note again. Touches the oilskin bag where it's been stapled shut. Closes his eyes; fast flash of his mirror-image from the Wall Dream. They blink open. Close again. American man's voice:* 'We can speak German if the English is giving you problems.'

Interior. DRITTEMANN *sits at a desk in an interview room facing his interviewer, behind whom is a large floor-length wall-mirror giving back the scene to itself. The interviewer is black, American, male, around Drittemann's age. His desk-name shines sternly under neon: Richard E. Davies. 2nd Consul.*
DRITTEMANN: English is not a problem.
DAVIES: (*In German*) . . . It's just that you haven't really answered any of my questions . . .
DRITTEMANN: (*In German; calm*) I know nothing, Mr Davies. I know nothing in German, I know nothing in English, I know nothing in American.
(DAVIES *sits back in his chair, studying Drittemann's file.* DRITTEMANN *watches the back of his head in the mirror.*)
DAVIES: Musician, says here. Taube Records. American and National. New York City. Visa to visit already applied for on your behalf by the company. I think it fair to warn you, Mr Drittemann, that US Immigration can be decisively influenced by our evaluation of the applicant. And in case you didn't know it, even the granting of a West German

passport is by no means automatic. It is already not in your favour that you were at one time a member of a communist organization; namely, the Young Pioneers . . .
(*He waits.* DRITTEMANN *sits impassively.*)
(*Flicking on*) Your sister defected to the West four years ago, is that right?
DRITTEMANN: Yes, that's what *I* heard.
(*Silence. They look at each other.*)
DAVIES: (*Unruffled*) I think we should meet again, Mr Drittemann. How about next . . . Tuesday? Same time.
DRITTEMANN: Next Tuesday. Fine.
(*He waits.* DAVIES *is studying the file again.*)
I go now?
DAVIES: Are you in touch with your father at all?
DRITTEMANN: (*Slow*) No.
(DAVIES *looks up carefully from the file. Nods.*)
LUCY: (*Voice over*) Klaus Drittemann, Rainer Schiff.

Exterior. Terrace café. DRITTEMANN's *eyes blink open.* SCHIFF, *six foot, bronzed, greying hair, in blue denim suit and good shirt, stands over him. A camera clicks.*

Exterior. Terrace café. The photographer, UWE, *bags his gear, session over.* LUCY BERNSTEIN *goes through other calls with him, diary in hand.* DRITTEMANN *and* SCHIFF *sit at table.* SCHIFF *signs an autograph book for a teenage girl, nods at the smiling mother some tables away.* DRITTEMANN *watches the gold ring, the gold pen.*
SCHIFF: (*Amused, ironic; in German*) I used to consider myself a quite good poet. A five-minute poorly lit appearance in a Herzog movie has cured me of all that . . . The only reason the West needs fewer instruments of repression is because it has learnt to calibrate seduceability. We are still unfree . . .
(LUCY *rejoins them, the photographer despatched.* SCHIFF *stands.*)
(*In American*) That my cab? Good. Lucy, think Connecticut. In the autumn. I'm crazy about the idea. (*To* DRITTEMANN, *in German, ironic*) I'll see you Thursday and listen, don't worry, depend on it, they'll let you back East

just as soon as you start earning real money . . . What you have to come to terms with, comrade, is that – compared to foreign exchange – mere ideology counts for nothing.
(*He tschusses his goodbyes, walks* LUCY *a few steps towards the road, kisses her cheek, leaves.* LUCY *returns to the table;* DRITTEMANN *counts out coins into a saucer.*)
LUCY: Harvard have offered him a visiting professorship for the fall . . . OK, that's it until tonight.
DRITTEMANN: Fine.
(*They sit in careful silence for a moment. She spreads a few black and white prints of a sombre* DRITTEMANN *in front of him.*)
LUCY: Like any of these?
(DRITTEMANN *looks, shrugs.*)
Uwe says he's waiting for the first smile. (*She passes him a slip of paper.*) That's the address for your sister – I think it's her work-place.
(*He takes it, says nothing.*)
How was your screening?
DRITTEMANN: I think the CIA liked me. They want to see me again. I was surprised to find I'd already applied for a visa.
LUCY: (*Unfazed*) I told you last night: A & N are ready to go all the way with you. Why make things difficult?
DRITTEMANN: (*Standing, collecting package*) What time's Braun?
LUCY: Eight.
DRITTEMANN: (*Moving*) OK.
LUCY: (*After him*) I'd like some pictures of you by the Wall sometime, what do you think?
DRITTEMANN: (*In German, leaving*) I don't think so . . .

Exterior. Afternoon. By Moritzplatz. DRITTEMANN, *package under arm, stares over wasteland at the Wall. Someone has sprayed 'Long Live Actually Existing Socialism!' across it in red.*

Exterior. U-Bahn. Evening. DRITTEMANN *stands jammed in a bay. It's rush-hour. He studies faces. Finds them strange; no lived experience in the eyes or mouths that he can share. He tries eye-contact; is refused, again, again. A man reads the* Berliner Zeitung am Abend: DRITTEMANN *scans it over his shoulder. Sees a pic of himself arriving at border control, kissing a greeting woman, handing her flowers.*

Interior. Ku'damm Clinic. Oberschwester's office. Point of view of six black and white monitors slung above a desk. Five of them show close-ups of female post-surgical patients' faces, two recent enough to be still gauzed. The sixth monitor, in looser shot, shows an anaesthetized woman being returned to her bed from a theatre trolley.

Two nurses and an Oberschwester complete the shift.
DRITTEMANN, *in close-up, scanning the images, hearing the low drifts of sound that bounce and slither across the open plan of the clinic.*
WOMAN: (*Out of shot, behind him, in German*) Klaus?
   (*He turns, sees the Oberschwester in the doorway, arms reaching for him.*)
DRITTEMANN: Hello, Mecki.
   (*They hug, friends, brother and sister. She's older by a couple of years.*)
DRITTEMANN: Long time.
MECHTHILD: I took my chance.
DRITTEMANN: (*Arm's length*) You look all right. What's this place?
MECHTHILD: Listen, thanks for coming, but I'm working . . .
DRITTEMANN: Well, where do you live, I'll come and see you . . .
MECHTHILD: Why don't I come and see you?
   (*They look at each other. She wonders whether to explain.*)
DRITTEMANN: You're the Oberschwester.
MECHTHILD: I'm having some problems with the man I live with . . . He can't decide whether he's a pig or a bunch of tulips. It's a problem he appears to share with most of his fellow countrymen . . .
DRITTEMANN: Same old Mecki.
MECHTHILD: (*A hard laugh*) Ha! (*She waves at the place she's in.*) You know what they do here? We? We give the rich new faces. New dreams. New possibilities. Costed by the millimetre. Same old Mecki? If I'd had real courage when I got here I'd've joined the Red Army Faction. Because here, you see, it's that or it's . . . this, or something like it . . . So: give me your number, leave it on the pad there . . . Are you OK?
   (DRITTEMANN *nods, grinning, happy with her.*)
   I still miss that place, you know. Shit, I really do.
   (*She watches him write down his number, hand it to her.*)
   How's mother?
DRITTEMANN: She's fine.

MECHTHILD: Still hate my guts?
DRITTEMANN: You know Rosa.
(*She nods. Turns away, to lead him out of the room.*)
Meck.
(*She turns.*)
I might need to see father. Any ideas?
MECHTHILD: Yes, that woman at Taube mentioned you were looking. I tried briefly just after I arrived. After a while it didn't seem important.
(*She walks him off down a long, perfectly reconstructed corridor towards the boulevard. Slips her arm into his. Hugs him a little.*)
DRITTEMANN: (*Voice over, German*) Let me speak to Herr Braun, please. (*Brief wait.*) Herr Braun?
(*Cut to:*)

Interior. Droysenstrasse apartment. Close-ish shot of the oilskin package on a table. DRITTEMANN's *hand enters the shot, begins to unstaple the neck and draw things out: a batch of letters and cards, maybe thirty, held inside an elastic band; a clutch of notebooks, journals, pads, diaries, snapshots, bound together by cloth tape; an open brown manila envelope from which the hand spills an assortment of musical compositions on music paper. The hand rummages, turns up, reveals, pauses over, the materials, seeking meanings, throughout the telephone exchange.*
DRITTEMANN: (*Voice over, German, room acoustic*) Herr Braun, Klaus Drittemann. Lucy Bernstein said I should . . .
BRAUN: (*Voice over, German, shrunken in the earpiece*) Herr Drittemann, thank you for calling, I just wanted to satisfy myself personally that everything was being done to make you welcome . . .
DRITTEMANN: Everything's fine, thank you.
BRAUN: Good. Excellent. We'll see each other Thursday night, of course, the welcome party . . . But if there's anything you need, don't hesitate, that's what we're here for . . . (*A small silence.*) The press conference . . . did Miss Bernstein mention the Culture Senator . . . Herr Hundhammer.
DRITTEMANN: (*Deadpan*) Herr Hundhammer? No, I'd've

remembered . . .

BRAUN: We can't announce this yet, of course, but there's a very good chance he'll turn up in person to make a brief speech of welcome and get the conference under way.
(*Silence. The hand rummages on. Turns over a clutch of musical compositions: 'Cantata for Peace in Our Time'; 'The Past Cannot Be Our Future'; 'Red Dawn'..*)

DRITTEMANN: (*Casually*) Wasn't he a fascist once? Herr Hundhammer?

BRAUN: (*Thrown*) A fascist? I rather doubt that. There was a Hundhammer founded the CSU once upon a time, quite possibly you're thinking of him . . .

DRITTEMANN: Quite possibly.
(*Silence. The hand probes on; reaches snapshots: of Jacob Drittemann the boy; the youth; the young man in Spain. Some are only half-pics, the rest cut away. There's a print of the black and white family portrait we've already seen on Rosa's bureau. Rosa has been neatly scissored from the shot.*)

BRAUN: (*Tentatively*) You saw the specimen contract I had drawn up?

DRITTEMANN: Yes.

BRAUN: Good. If there's anything you need to discuss, I'm at your disposal.

DRITTEMANN: Fine.
(*The hand reaches two ancient passports, one Austrian, one Dutch, both bearing Jacob Drittemann's name and picture. Close up of* DRITTEMANN, *frowning down at what he sees.*)

Interior. The Apollonia, Italian restaurant, West Berlin futuristic – white, clear plastic and glass furnishings and fittings; phones at each table. DRITTEMANN *and* LUCY BERNSTEIN *dine out in style at a large table, bedded in the Berlin of the Beautiful People. There are two places permanently free, at which people from other tables coast the main gathering, leaning in for the occasional discreet flash-pic. Over,* DRITTEMANN's *voice, in German:*

DRITTEMANN: Idea for a Song:
The Day They Took the Wall Away.
The day they took the Wall away –

Nothing happened.
The U-Bahn still flew above the housetops
Cars still sailed down the Spree
Nuclear stations went on protecting the atmosphere
Der Spiegel went on telling the truth
The CIA went on minding their own business
Fassbinder, though dead, went on making great German movies
Erich Honecker went on ignoring his appearance
And DDR citizens continued to exercise their democratic rights
The day after, a few snowdrops appeared,
The day after that, a crocus or two, a bluebell.
People stopped in the street to look,
Trying to remember their names.
(*Chords on a guitar. Sings:*)
The day they took the Wall away –
Nothing happened.
(DRITTEMANN *and* LUCY BERNSTEIN, *in loose shot. She watches him carefully.*)

LUCY: (*Sotto, casual*) Had enough?
DRITTEMANN: Oh yes.

Exterior. Night. The 190E draws up to the kerb outside the Droysenstrasse apartment. The engine is cut.

Interior. Car. LUCY BERNSTEIN *and* DRITTEMANN *sit in silence for a moment looking ahead into the half-dark of the leafy street.*
LUCY: (*Not the question*) Did you see your sister?
DRITTEMANN: Yes. (*Pause.*) She knows nothing.
LUCY: ?
DRITTEMANN: About my father. Where he is. If he is.
LUCY: Oh.
(*A police car noses by. One of the cops stares greenly at them, expressionless.*)
The Dutchwoman arrives tomorrow, perhaps she'll have something, I've arranged for her to be at Schiff's for the party.

(*He says nothing. Prepares to leave.*)
Is it important? Finding your father?
DRITTEMANN: (*Slow*) Perhaps. (*Inspects the question's intimacy; suspects it*) It's hard to say. (*He's leaving again.*)
LUCY: We need to speak about the contract, shall I come up? (DRITTEMANN *leaves his hand on the door handle, his eyes on the steps to the apartment.*)
DRITTEMANN: It's . . . in hand.
LUCY: The Chief wonders if you might need a lawyer to help you find your way through it . . . We'd be happy to suggest one . . .
DRITTEMANN: (*Opening door*) No. I think I can manage. (*He's on the pavement.*) Good night.
(*He smiles, formal, polite. Her lips are taut; control is an effort. She watches him let himself in the front door. Starts the car with a roar. Skids away.*)

Interior. DRITTEMANN *climbs the narrow stairs to his apartment door. Prison sounds clank in his head, stop abruptly as he sees the figure of a young woman curled up in his doorway, a rucksack clutched to her middle. He stands over her for a moment, then crouches to blow on her lidded eyes. The eyes open; see him.*
DRITTEMANN: (*In German*) Good evening.
WOMAN: Klaus Drittemann?
DRITTEMANN: (*German*) Who wants to know?
WOMAN: Emma de Baen.
DRITTEMANN: Ah.

Interior. Droysenstrasse apartment. EMMA, *mid-twenties, stands in the half-dark of the large living room, casually scanning the undisturbed contents of the table: contract, sleeve mock-ups, fan mail, bank statements, printed party invitation, the Dutch paper with her article and picture. She wears old blue jeans, combat jacket, T-shirt, short boots.*
DRITTEMANN *in from kitchen area carrying mugs of coffee and a plate of faded bread and cheese on a tray. She makes space for it on the table. Sets to, very functionally: cheese, brown bread, black coffee.* DRITTEMANN *takes his mug, sits on a stool in the darkness,*

watches her.

EMMA: (*In English*) You speak English?
DRITTEMANN: (*In German*) A little. Why? Don't you speak German?
EMMA: (*In German*) Yes. But I prefer not to.
(*He nods. She eats on. He waits for more. There is none. He lights a Marlboro.*)
DRITTEMANN: (*In English*) So. What about Jacob Drittemann?
EMMA: (*Eating; factual*) I think I've found him.
(*Silence.* DRITTEMANN *blinks in the shadows, dealing with an unexpected excitement. The woman begins to roll herself a cigarette.*)
Do you have a drink?
DRITTEMANN: Scotch?
(*She nods. He crosses to a cabinet, pours two, carries hers to the lit table, retires to his stool.*)
Think?
(*She carries her Scotch to a sofa, out of the light, squats on it, feet beneath her, as if unwilling to be part of the room. The light divides them.*)
EMMA: (*Rolling her amphora*) Your father gave his last public concert in 1971, made his last recording the same year, in Israel. There seems to have been a health problem, heart perhaps, it's vague. In early '72 he visited America, health again – New York in February, Washington in March. After that, nothing. Without trace. Gone. No one knows where. I have my notes . . . You can take it nothing has been overlooked.
(*He nods her on, held.*)
There is a man in Cambridge, England, of your father's age, calling himself James Dryden, to whom Philips International send half-yearly royalty payments, poste restante. Jacob Drittemann, who made two recordings with Philips in the early sixties, receives no royalty payments under that name. (*She lights the fine fag she's been rolling.*) There's more, but you have the bones of it. I think James Dryden is your father.
(*She watches him across the light; waits for his response. He*

stares back, wordless. She stands, removes two black and white prints from a wallet in her back jeans pocket, places them on the table. DRITTEMANN crosses to look. For a moment, man and woman are in the light. DRITTEMANN's gaze is blank, unrecognizing. In one, a sixty-year-old concert pianist stands on stage, left hand on piano, acknowledging applause.)
'69, Tokyo. Haifa, 1970. (Her finger indicates the same stranger, receiving an award.) When did you last see him?

DRITTEMANN: 1953. June 20th. I was six.
(EMMA *returns to her sofa, begins removing bits of gear from her rucksack.*)

EMMA: (*Not a question*) I'll stay the night, if that's all right . . .
(*He shrugs, nods.*)
There's no address, it's not even certain he's *living* as James Dryden, he may just have a bank account in that name . . . If you want him found, I'll have to go there. And since he's living incognito, it might help if you came too, to break the ice. Where's the bathroom?
(*He points, she carries her toothbrush out of the room, talking as she goes. He's drawn behind her in her wake.*)
I'll leave you a number where you can get me, I'll be here till . . . when's the press conference . . . Thursday? . . . Thursday, let me know what you want me to do, it needn't cost a lot, a couple of thousand marks, not more . . . (*She's in the bathroom, cleaning her teeth, looking at but not seeing the mirror over the basin.*) . . . Whatever you want . . .

DRITTEMANN: (*From passage by the doorway*) What tells you he's my father, this Dryden?
(*She spits into the bowl, looks at him.*)

EMMA: (*Clear*) My nose. It's my work. This is what I do.
(*She nudges the door closed, a slow exclusion.* DRITTEMANN *stares at it. Sounds of lavatory seat going down. Sounds of her beginning to piss.* DRITTEMANN *exchanges passageway walls, to rest his back against the doorjamb. Slowly turns the handle and nudges the door back open again, retiring for the linen cupboard along the passageway long before the seated woman profiled on the far wall has been inch by inch revealed.*)

DRITTEMANN: (*Out of shot*) I'll get you some bedclothes . . .

(The young woman's head jerks on the sound, sees the still-opening door, the empty passageway beyond. Cut in shot of retiring figure of DRITTEMANN *en route for the linen cupboard. She sits for a moment longer, stock still, one of the stockings from the shower-line in her hands. Cut to:)*

(Wall Dream). Colour. KLAUS DRITTEMANN *climbs a steep barbed-wired grass escarpment. Winds howl around the flattened top, where the man in the Tokyo picture beckons him to look East.* DRITTEMANN *stands upright. Blood trickles down his hands. He looks East, into the deep red sunrise. Is confronted with a vast outdoor drill area: a six-year-old boy in shorts and plimsolls, naked from the waist up, at attention, on punishment drill, alone in the centre, as the sun rises.*

Interior. Living room, Droysenstrasse apartment. Morning light slants angularly through curtained windows. Bedsheets on sofa thrown back, the woman gone. On the cushion pillow, a slip of graph paper with a Berlin telephone number crisply inscribed. Over this, fragments of press conference:
JOURNALIST: *(Woman; in German)* What about future plans, Herr Drittemann? I've heard rumours of a big tour and a new album for Christmas . . . Would you care to comment?

Exterior. Party at Schiff's. Just before dusk. Grünewald, Schlachtensee, around Marinesteig. The long green garden slopes gently down from the white detached house to the lake. Guests litter terraces, lawns and wooden jetty areas sprinkled with overhead party lights. From the bright house, full of people, the amplified sounds of Drittemann's 'In Praise of Nicaragua' drift across the company. DRITTEMANN *sits by the lake, Scotch in hand.* LUCY, RAINER SCHIFF *and others swim in the dark lake. He watches.* SCHIFF *calls him to join them. He raises his glass; sits on.* LUCY BERNSTEIN *wades out, joins him, begins to towel herself, limbs agleam in the dulling light.*
LUCY: You should try it. It's good.
(He says nothing.)
You saw your Dutchwoman then.

(*He hasn't mentioned it.*)
She rang me, she won't be here tonight . . . not her scene, she said. (*Beat.*) How is she?
DRITTEMANN: (*Thinking; then in German*) Strange. How did you come across her?
LUCY: (*In American*) She rang us. Just after we'd announced you'd been granted an exit visa. Said she was interested in doing a story on you and your father . . . Her credentials are good, she seemed just the person . . . How do you mean, strange?
DRITTEMANN: (*In English*) I don't know. (*Stares at her thighs as she rubs them.*) Maybe it's just West women.
(*A moment. A call from up the lawn. She looks away, up towards the house.*)
LUCY: (*In German*) Ah. The Chief . . .
(DRITTEMANN *stands to look.* WOLFGANG BRAUN, *young wife on arm, approaching, arm aloft in greeting, down the long lawn.* RAINER SCHIFF *arrives, struggling into a white robe and shaking his fine head.*)
SCHIFF: (*In German*) Hail, Caesar. Have you met your newest protégé . . . ?
(*Introductions, formal, German.* DRITTEMANN *studies the man, his own age, correct, a lawyer-manager, yellow-tint glasses and the lithe twenty-one-year-old model wearing his wedding band the only signs he's in the socially somewhat muddied waters of music production.*)
BRAUN: (*In German; producing a passport wallet from pocket*) Herr Drittemann, I take the very greatest pleasure in presenting you with your West German passport. May you live in peace and freedom among us.
(*A camera flashes, once, twice.* BRAUN *takes* DRITTEMANN'S *hand, gives it several strong clasps.* SCHIFF *applauds and bravos ironically.* DRITTEMANN *opens the wallet, studies the document.*)
DRITTEMANN: (*In German*) Thank you. I'm grateful. The CIA weren't so sure your government would grant it.
BRAUN: The CIA don't run everything here, Herr Drittemann . . .

DRITTEMANN: I'm glad to hear it. And the visa for America? (*He indicates it's not in the green book.*)

BRAUN: That takes a little longer. Show Renata the new Ambros tape, Rainer, she can't believe this new career of yours as a video-director . . . Lucy, call California, the Kristofferson–Grace Jones idea is active again, they want your thoughts on it today . . .
(*People are dispersed.* BRAUN *and* DRITTEMANN *remain. A boat bobs around out on the lake, a lamp in its bow. They watch it together, as the light fades on their faces.*)
Had a call from the Ministry: Herr Hundhammer proposes to be with us in person for tomorrow's press conference. (*Silence.* DRITTEMANN *puts a match to a Marlboro.*)
He'll make a small speech of welcome and leave. (*Beat.*) You need say nothing by way of reply. (*Beat.*) Indeed, staying calm is almost certainly the name of the game tomorrow . . . until you have your bearings. What shall we do about this contract? I was rather hoping we might have reached provisional agreement on it in time for the conference.
(*A waiter arrives with drinks. They help themselves. The waiter leaves.*)

DRITTEMANN: Are you a lawyer, Herr Braun?

BRAUN: I trained as a lawyer, yes.

DRITTEMANN: If you were my lawyer, what would you be advising me? *Vis-à-vis* the contract.

BRAUN: Sign. Unequivocally. It's an excellent deal. And you need Taube. We're the only independent left in Germany dealing with progressive music; we know the market you're in better than anyone; and CBS would eat you alive. How many reasons do you need, Herr Drittemann?

DRITTEMANN: Forgive my naïveté, Herr Braun. Knowing how to behave as a commodity isn't innate, you know, it has to be learnt. Up to now I have experienced it only in books, as a historical phenomenon widespread under capitalism, a thing of the past all my life. And it may take a little while, because before I can analyse your 'plans' for my 'exploitation' in 'the world's music markets' – I quote – I

need to know whether I can live and work properly here
. . . whether I have anything to say here . . .
(*A barrage of fireworks erupts suddenly across the lake. Party
people push down the lawn to watch. Slowly we read what the
explosions have written on the black air:* WELCOME.
Applause, much toasting, handshaking, shoulder-slapping.
DRITTEMANN *scans the crowding faces, harsh under the
electric lights; arrives at* LUCY's. *She's watching him intently.
Bring up sounds of Wolfgang Ambros: 'The Last Dance' ('Der
letzte Tanz') and mix very slowly through to Schiff's cold and
plastic-erotic video of the song's re-issue as a single.*)

Schiff's video. Cut in, unexplained, guests' faces, among them
DRITTEMANN's, *watching. The set they watch has one main and
four preview monitors showing three West German and two East
German programmes.*

*Interior. Another beautiful room. People watch a black American
male improvise a tenor-sax accompaniment to a woman
reciting/performing a poem.*
WOMAN: (*Australian, thirty*)
    So we left Peru, in a boat
    No bigger than Herzog's Volvo,
    And in the slick slither of moon
    That lit us forth, I found, before
    The four old cocks had chance to stiffen,
    A darling Key of Coke,
    On the rock, in a cupboard,
    Under a stairway, overlooked,
    Droppings from some larger deal.
    Six thousand miles they fucked me.
    Honolulu. (*Very long pause.*)
    Brisbane. (*Longer.*)
    The four old cocks.
    Six thousand miles I had my nose
    On the rocks . . .
(*The* TENOR's *stopped. She looks at him.*)
Something wrong?

TENOR: Any chance o' touchin' it, ma'am?
The nose, I mean . . . ?
(DRITTEMANN *laughs.* LUCY BERNSTEIN *watches him.*)

Interior. Dancing, eating, marijuana, spirits.

Interior. Large drawing room. DRITTEMANN *sings at the piano: 'Blues for a Red'. People sing with it.*

Interior. Black glass coffee table. RAINER SCHIFF *lays out lines of cocaine with a fine pen-knife.* KLAUS DRITTEMANN *watches. People sit or kneel around the Chinese carpet, waiting to snort:* FRAU BRAUN *does plenty, hands the straw to* LUCY, *who takes a line.* DRITTEMANN *watches. On the tape-deck, Randy Newman sings 'Guilty':*
> Got some whisky from the barman
> And some cocaine from my friends
> And I keep on moving, baby,
> Till I'm in your arms again.

Interior. Long, narrow kitchen. Dregs of the night slurry towards morning. RAINER SCHIFF *sits on a stool, smoking, drinking, talking, maundering.* DRITTEMANN *sits on a second stool several metres away, smoking, drinking, half listening. Between them, isolated from both, a young man of nineteen or twenty, slim, sullen, Audenesque blond hair, on another stool. Randy Newman:*
> Guilty
> I'm guilty
> And I'll be guilty for the rest of my life.
> How come I never do
> What I'm supposed to do . . .
> How come nothin' I try
> Ever turns out right.

(SCHIFF *joins Newman for the last verse, directing it at the young blond's dead beauty in profile.*)
> You know I'll harass you, baby,
> You know I just can't stand myself,
> It takes a whole lotta medicine, darling,

Interior. Press conference, Taube offices. The wall clock says 11.17. People wait, cough and shuffle through the hiatus. DRITTEMANN, BRAUN and BERNSTEIN at a raised table at the front; behind them, several huge pics of Klaus Drittemann in performance, hair flying. About two dozen journalists, cameramen and free-loaders occupy the remainder of the room.

JOURNALIST: (German) Shall we go on?

BRAUN: Please . . .

JOURNALIST: Yes, I'd like to ask about the haircut . . . Is this the new Klaus Drittemann in the West? . . . And what does it mean?
(Some chuckles. DRITTEMANN stares at the wild-haired pics behind him. Strokes his bristles.)

DRITTEMANN: Once, for a whole month, I had the longest hair in the DDR . . . and it was a statement. A meaning. (Rubs head again.) This? I feel like an exile. So I look like one.

For me to pretend I'm somebody else.
(The youth smiles briefly, at no one, exactly between the two men. SCHIFF *is erect, angry;* DRITTEMANN's *a bit slumped, carapaced by booze, studying his passport.)*

SCHIFF: *(Suddenly; German)* Damn your fascist eyes!
(The youth smiles again, again briefly. SCHIFF's *crying, soft improbable snuffs, tears greasing the face. In the doorway behind him,* LUCY BERNSTEIN *looms, some papers under her arm.* DRITTEMANN *sees her. She holds a car-key up. He nods.)*

Interior. Droysenstrasse apartment. Bedroom, streetlit.
DRITTEMANN *and* LUCY BERNSTEIN *fight naked on the bed, attempting love. They address each other in their respective languages occasionally, deep breathy barks, but mostly they bruise each other in silence. A bad fuck: trustless.*

Interior. Bedroom. LUCY BERNSTEIN *sits on the bottom of the bed, dressing in the dark room: left stocking, shoes, dress.* DRITTEMANN *lies flat on his back, a Marlboro in his lips, staring at the ceiling.*

DRITTEMANN: *(In English)* I told Braun, I tell you, I sign when I'm ready, when I know what I'm doing, what is to be done. OK? Next, the tour doesn't interest me, except perhaps for the gig in Zurich. I'll let you know. Next, I'm a *Liedermacher*; don't *ever* show me someone else's lyrics again. *(He has picked a ream of them up from the bedside table, hurls them down the room.)* Do me no favours, Miss Bernstein . . .
(She is dressed, ready, leaves. He stares at the ceiling for a while, a fist punching the wall behind his head. Over, press conference acoustic:)

BRAUN: Ladies and gentlemen, I have just been handed a message, the Culture Senator will be with us in a couple of minutes; he has, as we surmised, been unavoidably detained . . .

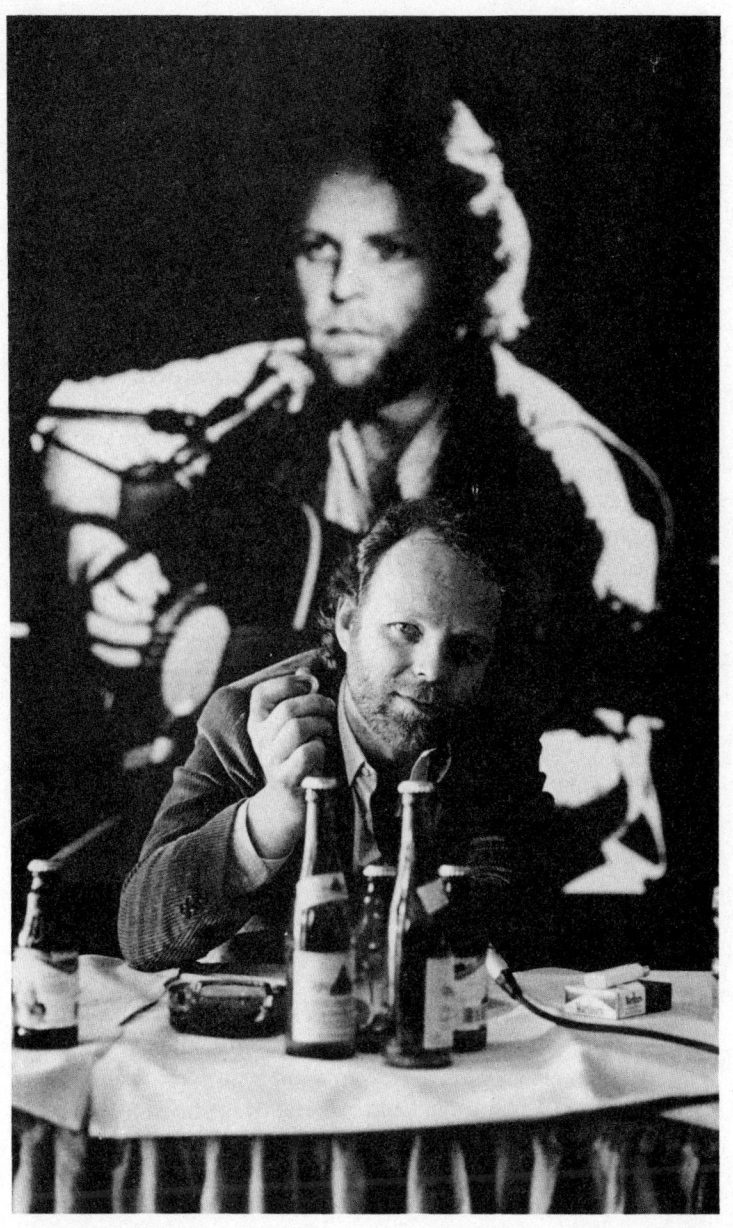

(*The swing doors push open and the Ministry men appear –* SENATOR HUNDHAMMER, *two assistants, two security. One security posts himself almost invisibly by the door. The remainder bull their way to the dais. Cameras whirr, click; people move to better vantage points.* BRAUN *greets* HUNDHAMMER, *who looks like Strauss's less attractive brother. Handshakes, introductions, as cameras flash and click.* HUNDHAMMER *takes out a page of notes and his glasses. Sits. His aides stand behind him.*)

HUNDHAMMER: Ladies and gentlemen . . . Apologies for lateness, we were detained at a previous engagement. It is my very great pleasure to extend the hand of welcome to Herr Drittemann . . .
(*He stands, extends the hand of welcome;* DRITTEMANN *stands, takes it. Cameras click into life.*)
The free city of West Berlin and the Federal Republic of Germany, in greeting you today, once more acknowledge the historic reality that Germans are Germans, wherever they are born, and that Germans who suffer under an oppressive system will never find our door closed to them.
(*He stares over his reading glasses at the assembled throng, as he prepares to detach from the text.* DRITTEMANN *looks at* BRAUN, *who shrugs, indicates he should stay cool.*)
I'm told that Herr Drittemann, despite his treatment, is still something of a leftist and that the songs he writes here may well be critical of the CDU government. Well, as in a very minor way a member of that government, I say to him: feel free, that is your prerogative. Indeed the louder you shout, the larger your subsidy, very often. (*Laughter.*) May your music flourish, Herr Drittemann. And may you live in peace and freedom all your days.
(HUNDHAMMER *pouches his glasses, pockets his notes, nods to his aides, shakes* BRAUN's *hand and departs.* DRITTEMANN's *voice, on mike, arrests his progress half-way down the room.*)
DRITTEMANN: I thank the Culture Senator for his words of greeting, but would remind him that citizens of the DDR do not require lessons on freedom and its uses from those who stand in the direct line of German Fascism. My quarrel

with the government of my country is my business and will
be settled between us. Under no circumstances will I allow
it to be collapsed into a reactionary capitalist critique of
post-capitalist society. And I would remind the Culture
Senator that oppression comes in many guises: tolerance is
one of them; the whole apparatus of secret surveillance and
Berufsverbot another. 'Peace and freedom' courtesy of the
CIA and the *Verfassungsschutz* – both of whom are almost
certainly represented at this gathering here today – may
satisfy the Culture Senator and his kind but they should
never be confused with real peace and real freedom,
especially in 1986 . . .
(*The room has brewed up into chat and comment, as*
DRITTEMANN's *dry and precise passion discharges itself. Aides
lean in to urge calm on* HUNDHAMMER: *he shrugs them aside,
eager for battle.*)
HUNDHAMMER: Feel free, Herr Drittemann. Say what you will.
Taste freedom. And sleep safe in your bed. You make my
point.
(*He wheels, leaves. Several journalists applaud. A few set up a
counter-hiss.* DRITTEMANN *lights a Marlboro; sees* EMMA DE
BAEN *enter the doorway* HUNDHAMMER *and his entourage
have just cleared. The conference is in considerable disarray.*)

Interior. Braun's suite of offices and passageway. DRITTEMANN
*paces the corridor, smoking, staring out of the window at the
Ku'damm below. From within the suite of offices, the disjointed
sounds of several telephone conversations:* BRAUN's, LUCY
BERNSTEIN's, *others. They're checking with journalists on how
things have been received.*
LUCY BERNSTEIN *appears in the passageway. Approaches*
DRITTEMANN, *who continues staring out of the window.*
LUCY: I think we're winning. On the whole they seem to have
liked your style. But it's a close thing.
(DRITTEMANN *looks at her. Looks away again.*)
(*Honeymoon over*) Herr Braun will see you in five minutes.
He needs a decision on the contract. Yes. No.
(*She goes back into the offices.* DRITTEMANN *stubs his*

cigarette. *Begins an aimless wander around the corridors. Glass cases announce prize-winning discs; posters proclaim bands under contract.*
He reaches the conference suite, still strewn with the morning's detritus. EMMA DE BAEN *sits at the back of the room, as if waiting for him. They stare at each other for several moments. Pick of telegraph keys starts up.*)

Interior. Train. Close up of DRITTEMANN, *watching fields flow past.*
Caption: *Stalinism is not socialism.*
         Capitalism is not freedom.
Over, the cable in his voice: Searching for peace and freedom stop. Maybe Zurich stop.
He turns his gaze into the carriage. EMMA DE BAEN *sits at the opposite window. They regard each other.*

Interior. LUCY BERNSTEIN *at her office desk. Night. She studies the cable under bright Anglepoise.*
DRITTEMANN: (*Voice over*) Contract on way stop. Drittemann.
(*She lays the cable to one side. Under it, the contract. She studies each of the six quarto sheets: all fourteen clauses have been struck out. On the final page, Drittemann's signature.*)

Interior. Night. Railway carriage. DRITTEMANN *sits by a window, back to engine, the opened oilskin package on his knees, studying documents. He wears Max's black leather belted overcoat.*
DRITTEMANN: (*Voice over, German*) 'Berlin, 20th July, 1953. Rosa. When you read this I shall already be in the West. Whatever you may think you know, whatever you may imagine to be the case about me, I beg you to accept that none of it was planned or foreseen. Since Spain – before, perhaps – my principal shaping forces have been . . . haphazardness; and a sort of terrible innocence. I do not so much *do* as find myself doing. To the charge of innocence I must plead guilty. Venial enough, you would think; and yet here I am, dishonoured in your eyes, and forcibly removed from the lives of my children. No doubt I'll survive it all;

but for *what* I cannot at the moment imagine . . .'
(DRITTEMANN *looks away from the page, uncomfortable with it. Sees* EMMA DE BAEN *watching him from the seat opposite. The train is slowing. Dogs bark up the track. Calls of 'Helmstedt' and 'Border control' from corridor.*)

Interior/exterior. DRITTEMANN's *corridor window-view of the border point some way up the track. Armed border guards make their way down the line, German shepherd dogs on stout leashes, searching beneath the train for East German stowaways.*
MAN'S VOICE: (*Behind him, out of shot*) Passport.
(DRITTEMANN *turns, a touch startled. A border guard has approached down the corridor.* DRITTEMANN *hands him the document.*)
GUARD: Ticket. (*He looks at each several times, then once, quite searchingly, at* DRITTEMANN, *before handing them back.*) Take your seat, please.
(DRITTEMANN *thinks of replying, thinks better of it, returns to his seat. The* GUARD *studies Emma de Baen's passport and ticket.* DRITTEMANN *and* EMMA *exchange a look. Outside, a dog barks, a man's voice snarls it quiet.*)

Exterior. Hoek van Holland. Noonish. DRITTEMANN *and* EMMA *queue for the boat to Harwich, swamped in a sea of British squaddies en route for Britain and their summer leave. The air seethes with aggression, chauvinism, psychosis in uniform. A great cheer goes up as a Union Jack's waved by someone on the boat they're boarding.*

Exterior. Day. At sea. DRITTEMANN *makes a careful way through drunken, largely prone, soldiery, two cans of beer in his hands. A flattened squaddie vomits over the mate who's helping him to his feet.*

Exterior. Day. Upper deck, prow end. DRITTEMANN *hands a can to* EMMA, *sits in the chair beside her. The deck is dense with lumpen khakied forms glugging, snorting, shouting, moaning, wobbling, falling. Empty Johnny Walker half-bottles get hurled seawards; some smash against rails. A massy simian Scot, more tattoo than*

skin, sits on someone's suitcase, calling the odds from the depths of his whiskied stupor.
SOLDIER: A'll fait any fucka here, awrait? Krauts, frogs, tulips, wops, wogs, the fuckin' lot o'ye.
(He glares around him. Eyes shift, avoiding contact. He fixes on DRITTEMANN, *who stares back at him.)*
What're you? Fuck'n Kraut're ye? Shoulda fuck'n bombed youse lot te fuck in the last lot, that's what we shoulda done. (*A slow deep suck on the Bell's half in his hand.*) We'll fuck'n show ye . . . (*Stabs a finger at the ribbon on his chest.*) Falklands. Falklands. See it. S'just the start, that, eh? Mmm? (*Blinks, half blind with booze.*) Ye wanna fait, jummy?
(DRITTEMANN *has understood nothing, save the hard hate in the voice and the despair below it.*)
Phaa.
(*The* SCOT *tries to stand, clawing at his flies. A slow, dark stain spreads from the crotch to the knees of his coarse khaki trousers. The man watches it uncomprehendingly for some moments, then tries to resume his seat on the suitcase, misses, and collapses on to the deck; gone.* EMMA DE BAEN *says something in Dutch to* DRITTEMANN, *who searches for her meaning.*)
EMMA: (*In English*) I said: he should help you sleep more safely in your bed.
(*Long shot of the top deck,* DRITTEMANN *and* EMMA *marooned in the midst of the military mayhem.*)

Exterior. Shot of ship's name: St Crispian.

Interior. Late afternoon. Customs shed, Harwich. We follow the two through a hard-faced immigration area, VDUs flashing, past a long line of black families confronting the joyless and unwelcome face of official Britain on its borders. Kids yawn, skrike, rub grubby fists into tired eyes; sari-ed women try to cope; husbands stand, solitary, doleful.

Caption: *Camp Freedom.*

Interior. Customs shed. The two stand at a trestle table in Green, having their bags and effects searched. DRITTEMANN, *repacking, watches Emma's battered leather satchel being rummaged: socks, tights, pants, wash-bag, files, documents, and a largish hardback book. He studies the title covertly, recognizing it:* Brown Book. *She flicks a look at his stare, restores the book to its bag. The Customs officer opens a heavy roundish package in distinctive red wrapping paper, uncovers a full Gouda cheese inside.*

Exterior. Harwich harbour. DRITTEMANN *stands amid the baggage, watching* EMMA *signing for the hire-car in a glass-fronted Avis office across the way. A Honda Civic is slowly driven up and parked in front of the window, partially blocking his view. A ship's horn sounds.* EMMA's *head jerks up at the blast; she sees* DRITTEMANN *watching her.* DRITTEMANN *looks away, up the slip-road. Two police cars stand bumper to bumper. The uniformed policemen, four of them, sit in one car.*

Exterior. Evening, around sunset. M11. EMMA *drives the Honda Civic,* DRITTEMANN *beside her. A local radio chat-and-music show has the local USAF Camp Commandant as studio guest. He explains the especial interest taken by the American Base in the life of the community (Christmas parties, Open Days, Fun Runs for local charities, a full educational programme for local schools free of charge . . .) A woman calls in to ask if he'd care to say anything about the sixty-four cruise missiles said to be already installed in his base. The chat show host intervenes, reminds the caller that the Commandant is not at liberty to discuss military and defence arrangements. Music up fast, another of the Commandant's favourites: Pat Boone's 'Friendly Persuasion'.* DRITTEMANN's *hand clicks it off at speed.*
Ahead, a lit road sign looms: Newmarket, Cambridge, Huntingdon, straight on. Services, one mile.

Interior. Motorway café. Vestibule, stiff with junk: shops, hot-dog stall, video-games, pinball, phone carousels. DRITTEMANN *pays for the dogs and Cokes, carries them out of the building and back to the car. It's empty. He looks around, checking it's the right one, deposits her food and drink on the dash, walks back towards the café. Sees* EMMA *ahead to the left, in the third of five outdoor glass phone-cabins, speaking into the telephone. He tucks himself casually into the dark of a wall. Watches, tight-eyed, eating the dog.*

Exterior. Night. Car headlamps pick out a country-road approach to Cambridge. Trees gleam silver in the light.
EMMA: (*Voice over, out of shot, factual*) . . . I booked accommodation before I knew you would come; so there's one room only, at least for tonight. What do you think?
(*The road unwinds ahead in the lamps.*)
DRITTEMANN: (*After thought, voice over, out of shot*) Let's hope it's a double. You know where you're going?
EMMA: (*Voice over, out of shot*) There's a street map in my satchel there, take it out . . .
(*He reaches behind, removes the map-book from the leather satchel. We see the red parcel next to it on the seat.*)
Address on the front there, see it?
(*The road goes on unravelling. Cottages appear sporadically, the promise of larger settlement looming. A road sign announces Cambridge and the town it's twinned with.*
Just beyond it, a loose indian file of youths walking home casually bare buttocks to the advancing light. The lamps swerve, to give them berth.)
(*Dutch*) Jesus Christus.
(*Shot of* DRITTEMANN, *looking back into the darkness.*)
DRITTEMANN: (*Quietly*) Willkommen?

Exterior. Night. Cambridge. A police patrol car nudges gently down a Victorian street of boarding houses. The non-driver radios in the numbers of parked cars. The car stops abreast of the Honda Civic: within thirty seconds it's been identified as an Avis hire car from Harwich. The patrolman writes something down in his notebook.
PATROLMAN: What's that, French? Dutch. Ahunh. Spell it, will you.

Interior. Night. Largish attic room: a miscellany of double bed, old three-piece suite, darkwood folding table, standing lamps.

DRITTEMANN *sits in a chair, studying his father's memorabilia spread on the oilskin between his feet, sipping Scotch from a half-bottle. A woman unloads a tray of cocoa and cheese sandwiches at the table, talking loud and incessant across alien space.*

LANDLADY: (*Forties, East Anglian*) Nice little nightcap, send you on your way, we like to make people welcome in this part of the world, all sorts we get here, all shapes and sizes, Japanese, Americans, Germans, a lot of French, it's the colleges you know, the buildings, that'll be three pounds eighty . . .
(DRITTEMANN *frowns, fiddles for his notes and change.*)
(*Nicely*) Oh, and fifty pence for your wife's bath, that'll be four pounds thirty altogether. Four pounds thirty. Have you finished with the phone book?
(*He nods; pays her. She leaves, directory in hand.*
DRITTEMANN *crosses to the table, picks at the plate of food, scans the spread street map, the red paper package and the leather satchel beside it. We read the label on the package:* 'James Dryden, Poste Restante, Head Post Office, Cambridge. To be collected.' *Slowly he slides the brown book from the satchel, opens it at the title page. The two pics of his father stare up at him, slightly obscuring the uncompromising title:* Brown Book: War and Nazi Criminals in West Germany. *Women's voices from the landing. He returns the book to its bag. Resumes his chair.*
EMMA *comes in, in tracksuit, towel over head. Sees the food. Helps herself. Sits on the bed to dry her hair.*)

EMMA: Is he listed?
(DRITTEMANN *shakes his head.*)
So. Tomorrow we begin. You found the post office?
(*He nods, sitting back to watch her, bottle to lips.*)
Good. I must sleep.
(*She turns some lights out, drinking her cocoa, climbs into the sheets, clicks out the bedlight, settles.* DRITTEMANN *sits on, head back, gaze on spidered ceiling. Over, parts of his father's letter again:* 'Berlin, 20th July, 1953. Rosa . . . Haphazardness. And a sort of terrible innocence. I do not so much do as find myself doing . . .')

(*Quiet*) Good night.
DRITTEMANN: (*Eventually*) Good night.

Interior. Attic room. Later. EMMA *sleeps on her back, tracksuit top discarded.* DRITTEMANN *stares down at her, unfastening his shirt. Sees the tattoo on her right shoulder: a red rose clenched like a fist.*

Interior. Attic room. Overhead shot. They lie on their backs. His eyes are open.

Interior. Sub-post office, Madingley. EMMA *watches the counter clerk weigh the red package.*

Exterior. DRITTEMANN *waits in the Honda.*

Interior. Sub-post office. The CLERK *tears stamps from his book, fixes them to the parcel.*
CLERK: You'd be better off taking this, you know, it's only down the road . . .
EMMA: How much?
CLERK: Two eighty.
   (*She pays, takes her receipt, leaves. The clerk lifts the package, feels it carefully, wrinkles his nose, sniffs the package, places it in a sack hung from the back wall.*)

Exterior/interior. Honda, entering Cambridge. Great colleges float by, six centuries of privilege in a single street. Gowned students pedal and pose across the day; tourists in clusters swell and thin like geese.
DRITTEMANN *misses nothing.* EMMA *pays no heed.*

Exterior. They approach the main post office on foot. Enter.

Interior. They approach the long counter. Reach the grille.
EMMA: Poste restante, please.
CLERK: Name?
EMMA: Renée Schoukendijk.
   (*The* CLERK *sifts letters in a cubby-hole; checks several packets in another. Shakes his head.* EMMA *smiles, retires with*

DRITTEMANN *towards the doorway. She stops a moment, watching the flow of traffic inside the large, busy room, as she notes down the office's hours of opening.)*

Interior. Woolworth's. They try on hats, sunglasses. Buy T-shirts and a variety of different tops.

Exterior. They sit by the Cam with their haul. DRITTEMANN *tries on his several hats, seeking the essential character of each.* EMMA *rolls a cigarette.*

EMMA: We'll do two-hour watches . . . Any longer and we'll be noticed.

(DRITTEMANN *replaces a trilby with a straw boater. She regards it a moment.*)

That's a mistake.

DRITTEMANN: (*Touching boater*) This? (*He gazes around him at*

  the blessed and lazy day.) Where were you trained?
EMMA: (*Quiet*) Trained?
DRITTEMANN: Maybe it's all a mistake. (*He waves his hand at
  Cambridge. Stares at the sky.*)

Sequence of post office watches and free time, favouring
DRITTEMANN. *Hats, tops and jackets casually inflect appearance
over the two or three days of the surveillance. Tension builds,
particularly for* DRITTEMANN. *He watches intently as old men
mumble their needs across the counter; scans faces; examines voices.*
EMMA DE BAEN *does her watches impassively, professionally
invisible in the constrained public space.*
Interspersed with watches, DRITTEMANN's *aimless scanning strolls
around the town throw up an essential imagery of a rotten Britain:
King's College Chapel choristers progressing down the street; skins on
the town; punks at corners; paired police; NF slogans; dole queues;
banks, churches; bad TV in pubs; dossers and dogs picking a
decorous way through the Bentleys and Mercedes. Once, we find him
testing a synthesizer keyboard in a high street music shop.*
DRITTEMANN *and* EMMA *are seen together only when one relieves
the other on counter-watch, when a tiny gestural intimacy charts the
developing relationship.*
Binding all this, a single boy chorister sings 'Happy Land':
  Happy land! happy land!
  Is now the chaunt in every street.
  Happy land! happy land!
  Sings everyone you meet.
  The ballad-singer, minus clothes,
  Shirtless, coatless, and
  With buckets none to shield his toes,
  He warbles 'Happy land!'

  Happy land! happy land!
  Exclaims the swell, reduced in pelf;
  To the parish workhouse goes,
  Where the official elf
  Who no humanity e'er owns,
  Commands him to depart,

Gives him a ticket to break stones
Or drag a water cart.

Happy land! happy land!
Cries, perhaps, a hungry group;
A cook shop view with longing eyes,
For a good blow-out of soup.
On each hot joint their eyes do dwell,
Bowels yearning, there they stand.
Then walk away – their share a smell –
And warble 'Happy land!'

Happy land! happy land!
Ne'er from thee I wish to stray,
The soldier cries, because, d'ye see,
He cannot get away.
For nothing flogged, with grief he sighs,
While probably the band
Strike up to drown the wretch's cries,
To the tune of 'Happy land!'

Happy land! happy land!
Thy fame resounds from shore to shore;
Happy land! where 'tis a crime,
They tell us, to be poor.
If you shelter cannot find,
Of you they'll soon take care;
Most likely send you to grind wind
For sleeping in the air.

Happy land! happy land!
To praise thee who will cease?
To guard us, pray, now ain't we got
A precious New Police?
A passport we shall soon require,
Which by them must be scanned,
If we to take a walk desire –
Oh, ain't this happy land?

Exterior. DRITTEMANN, *a long narrow cardboard box under an arm, a Sainsbury's plastic bag in his hand, approaches the post office, as a church clock sounds four. He checks his watch against the bell, enters the darkish place, stands adjusting his eyes for a moment, scanning the busy counters for signs of Emma de Baen. Fails to find her. Steps outside again. Searches the pavement. Goes back inside, frowning. Begins to cover his presence with process, filling in a motor vehicle licence form. In close-up, we see the tension mount. He checks his watch again; screws up the form; leaves the post office.*

Exterior. He approaches the boarding house, past the parked Honda, enters by the front door.

Interior. DRITTEMANN *stands in silence outside the door of the attic room. Goes in.*

Interior. EMMA DE BAEN *crouches over his bag, searching for something. Turns as he enters.*
EMMA: (*Calm*) Hi.
DRITTEMANN: Hi.
EMMA: (*Showing one in her hand*) I'm looking for a pen to leave you a note . . .
DRITTEMANN: Ahunh. (*He places the cardboard package and the shopping bag on the table, sees her Pentel there.*)
EMMA: That's dead.
DRITTEMANN: Ahunh.
EMMA: It's gone. Someone came for it.
(*Long silence.* DRITTEMANN *crosses to the window, looks out a moment.*)
DRITTEMANN: Him?
EMMA: A woman. I followed her home. It's just outside the town.
DRITTEMANN: Did you see him? Is he there?
EMMA: I saw nothing. A woman and a house. Come, I'll take you.
DRITTEMANN: Wait. (*He looks at her carefully.*) Sit down. There's time.
(*She pockets the car keys, sits at the table. He sits opposite, not quite facing her. He picks up the Pentel, spreads the street map between them.*)
Show me.
(*She studies the map, diffidently traces a route out of the city, rests her nail on its eastern edge.*)
You have the address?
(*She blinks. Looks at him. Takes out a notebook from her back pocket, tears out a page, hands it to him. He studies it.*)
Thank you.
EMMA: (*Calm*) What's the problem?
DRITTEMANN: I don't know. I sense . . . (*taps his nose, unconsciously echoing her*) something wrong. Bad. I think you should go back to Holland. Your work's finished.
(*She sits in silence for some time, watching him fiddle with the Pentel. The day has dulled outside the window. Light leaks from the room. He unpacks a Casio MT-40 synthesizer from the*

cardboard box, checks batteries, plays the melody line of 'In Praise of Nicaragua' in electric flute mode.)

EMMA: Fine. You're the boss.

DRITTEMANN: Am I?

EMMA: What do you mean?

(*He takes a half-bottle of Bell's from the shopping bag, empties two teacups into a teapot and pours for both.*)

DRITTEMANN: I sense, to tell truth, an interest in finding my father that has nothing to do with me. I sense: another master.

(*He holds his cup up, cool, remote. Drinks. She waits; calm, impassive.*)

Suddenly it occurs to me: a man does not hide who does not fear discovery. Dryden, Drittemann, it's all one . . . political folk are never safe this side of the grave . . .

EMMA: You think I'm working for some . . . what? . . . some . . . intelligence service? Some . . . Who?

DRITTEMANN: It doesn't matter who. I prefer not to think . . .

EMMA: You asked me to help you find . . .

DRITTEMANN: (*Hard*) You offered before I asked, you knew he needed 'finding' before I knew it myself, you even knew where he is, you needed me only to confirm it . . . No deal.

(*Their cold heat hangs between them in the room. He pours more whisky. She sips in silence, thinking.*)

Why do you carry a copy of the *Brown Book*? Are you a fascist?

EMMA: (*Fast, in Dutch*) Go and fuck yourself.

(*Silence. She rolls a cigarette. He studies her anger.*)

DRITTEMANN: What, then?

(*She lights the cigarette. Blows out the match. Looks at him.*)

EMMA: In 1942 my mother, age sixteen, and thirteen members of her family were rounded up by Nazis and sent to the death camps. Her father and mother, grandparents, uncles, aunts, cousins. All died, save her. She was nineteen when Ravensbruck was liberated; she weighed twenty-five kilos. It was another five years before she could stand upright and face the world again. And what she found was that most of those responsible, the Nazis, were back in high office again,

lawyers, judges, administrators, teachers, businessmen, as though nothing had happened. Indeed, nothing had happened: to them. She (*feels for the words*) . . . decided to do something about it. She married a man with money and used it to set up an agency . . . to bring them to justice. I work for her.
(*She sips her whisky.* DRITTEMANN *sits very still for some moments, absorbing her meanings, barely able to make her face out in the gloom. Clicks on the tablelamp, looks at her again.*)

DRITTEMANN: Jacob Drittemann was a communist. Fought in the Spanish Civil War. Served for seven years in the Ministry of Culture in the DDR. Fought Stalinism every day of his life. While Stalin lived. Left in protest at the brutal suppression of the Workers' Uprising by armed militia. And lives on to this day in the hearts of the socialist opposition there. (*Pause.*) What can any of this have to do with my father?
(EMMA *reaches for her leather sack, takes out a thickish file, places it on the table.*)

EMMA: There's two years' work there. Open it.
(*He opens it slowly. The first page has the original print of the blurred man in a field we first saw in her newspaper article.*)
Between Spain and America, your father spent several months in Holland, fighting with the Dutch Underground. Did you know?
(*He shakes his head.*)
In the town of Gouda. I found it in an archive. About a dozen German comrades took that route. One of them led a whole detachment of Resistance workers, twenty-eight men and twelve women, to their deaths in a Nazi ambush. Your father may have known the traitor. I have to ask him.
(*Silence. A knock at the door.*)

LANDLADY: (*Outside*) Mrs de Baen, are you there?

EMMA: (*Not moving*) What is it?

LANDLADY: (*Outside*) I wonder if you'd mind moving your car, it's blocking the driveway . . .

EMMA: Certainly.
(*She sits on for a moment. Leaves.*

DRITTEMANN *pours more whisky. Stares at the open dossier. Crosses to his bag. Removes the oilskin package; opens it; studies the Dutch passport. Returns to the table. Stares at the picture of the man in the field. Uncaps the Pentel. Draws the point across the map several times. It's spent. Flicks the dossier on, studying pictures, disarmed by the impenetrably Dutch text.* EMMA *returns. Sits in her chair at the table. Begins rolling another cigarette. He says nothing.*)

EMMA: So. Do I go home?

DRITTEMANN: I don't know.

(*He lights her cigarette. Lights one for himself. They smoke, drink, intimate suddenly. He reaches for the street map. Studies it through the smoke of his Marlboro.*)

Exterior. Night. DRITTEMANN *sits in the Honda, staring at a small undistinguished bungalow on a country road. A small lamp burns in one room. He watches. Broods.*

Interior. Attic room. He stands in the milk-dark room staring down at the bed. EMMA DE BAEN's *eyes open suddenly, focus at once. Silence.*

DRITTEMANN: All right.

EMMA: Thanks.

DRITTEMANN: But I see him alone.

EMMA: Of course.

(*He undresses in the darkness, slides into the bed. They lie on their backs, eyes open.*)

You saw the house?

DRITTEMANN: Poor bastard.

EMMA: Who?

DRITTEMANN: Dryden.

(*She says nothing.*)

I don't want him to be my father.

Exterior. Day. They sit in the Honda, watching the house. A woman, around fifty, shepherds two girls in school uniform into a Morris Traveller parked in the drive. The car takes off towards town. EMMA *nods.* DRITTEMANN *gets out of the Honda, begins to circle the house, scanning for signs of life.*

Exterior. DRITTEMANN *stands at the end of a long thin strip of garden, peering through a hedgerow at the back of the lifeless house. The garden is kempt but ordinary. Nothing stirs.*

Brief montage of the vigils over a couple of days, sometimes together, sometimes DRITTEMANN *alone and brooding. The woman returns from school pick-up in the late afternoon.* EMMA *notes down the woman's leaving and return times methodically.* DRITTEMANN *scans the house from an adjacent field. Sees a man's form cross a window once and disappear.*

Exterior. They sit in the car in a nearby lane, tucked under trees, with a different view of the driveway. The woman appears from the house, piles gear into the back, returns to the house, gives her arm to a gaunt old man swaddled to the neck in a travelling rug, helps him into the rear seat. EMMA *starts up the car.* DRITTEMANN *wipes steam from the windscreen, needing to see.*

Exterior. Via Devana. Two cars whirr across country, a furlong apart. A long army convoy passes them in the opposite direction. Ahead, three Hawker Hunters lance at imagined targets, a bare three hundred feet above them.

Exterior. Molesworth Base. A high-powered lens picks out women's faces. The women sing. The camera scans, clicks, freezes, scans on.

Exterior. A glade of high trees fringing the wire perimeter of a USAF base. The two cars are parked, a hundred yards apart. Women's voices sing, distant: 'Give Peace a Chance'.

Exterior. Shot through Honda windscreen of the Morris Traveller. The old man leans, slightly hunched, through the back passenger window.
EMMA: *(Voice over)* What's he doing?
　　(DRITTEMANN *leaves the car, crosses in front of it, crabs slowly through trees, trying to close on the other car. Gradually,*

still at unrecognizable distance, the OLD MAN *comes into view. He holds a long-lens camera out of the window, in the direction of the singing women.* DRITTEMANN *looks ahead, sees a circle of seated women outside the main gate of the base, a line of police opposing them: a still, iconic moment.*
A car door slams. The WOMAN *has left the Traveller, stretches her legs, smokes a cigarette, begins to wander in Drittemann's direction.* DRITTEMANN *stays very still. The* WOMAN *stops about twenty yards away; stands in her vacancy. She wears a jacket, wool skirt, silk headscarf, good shoes. Suddenly sees him. They look at each other. Neither speaks. She turns, walks back to the car.* DRITTEMANN *watches her say something to the* OLD MAN. *The car starts up, drives away.*)

Exterior. DRITTEMANN *waits for the approaching Honda, opens the door, leans in.*
EMMA: Get in.
DRITTEMANN: Let them go.
  (*She slips the car into neutral, releases the clutch. He climbs in beside her.*)
EMMA: (*Carefully*) You saw him?
DRITTEMANN: No.
EMMA: Then we should be following . . .
DRITTEMANN: (*Hard*) Where's he going to *go*? Let him be.
  (*She says nothing. Sits in tense silence.* DRITTEMANN *lights a Marlboro.*)
  Let's go.
  (*She looks at him. Puts the car into gear.*)
EMMA: He's not God. He's just your father.

Wall Dream. Black and white. Unsynched, intermittent sound. A glade of high trees. DRITTEMANN *flees, pursued, a Sainsbury's plastic shopping bag in his hand, guitar slung across his back. The trees thicken, the path grows less certain. A huge earthwork confronts him. He turns, listens. Shot of German shepherd dogs, snouts to the ground, soldiers' leather boots a step behind them, driving forward.* DRITTEMANN *attacks the earthwork, clawing for the top. Arrives,*

exhausted; lies, face to earth, for some time. Something creaks, swinging, a distance away along the rampart. He looks up. Ahead, the lifeless body of the old man hangs by the feet from a wooden telegraph pole. Blood from the nose and mouth trickles into the open eyes. The face smiles. DRITTEMANN's *mouth opens.*
A screaming cry.

Interior. Attic. Night. DRITTEMANN *sits upright in the dark bed, shouting in German.* EMMA *calms him. He lies back on the pillow. She clicks on a light.*
EMMA: Are you ill?
DRITTEMANN: It's nothing. Dreams.
　(She studies his face. Dabs the sweat from it with a tissue.)
EMMA: *(Gentle)* Do you want anything?
　(He looks at her. She holds the stare. She says a word in Dutch. The looks hold.)
　(Finally) Unschuld. *(Pause.)* Innocence? *(Pause.)* You're discovering the West has no use for it either. Sleep.
　(She turns out the light. Settles on her back next to him. He lights a cigarette.)
DRITTEMANN: *(Finally, from the dark)* How long do we have the car?
EMMA: Friday.
　(The cigarette glows and dies in the blackness.)
DRITTEMANN: Tomorrow then.
EMMA: All right.

Interior. Day. Attic window. DRITTEMANN *looks down at the leaden street. Recent rain still pocks the panes. The Honda arrives.* EMMA *winds the window down, stares up at him.*
DRITTEMANN *leaves the dormer-hollow, collects his black leather overcoat and the Sainsbury's bag from the armchair, leaves.*

Exterior. Windscreen view of the Dryden drive, through passing traffic. The Morris Traveller waits to join the road; finds space; fills it, heading for the town. The two girls in the back are happy, boisterous.

Exterior. DRITTEMANN *gets out of the Honda, stares at the bungalow.* EMMA *calls him.*
EMMA: (*Out of shot*) Klaus.
>(*He leans back into the car. She opens the glove compartment, hands him a pack of Marlboro.*)
>Don't forget these . . . They had only one packet.
>(*He takes them, puts them in his pocket.*)
>You have an hour. Good luck. (*Indicating*) I'll be that way . . .
>(*He nods. Closes the door. The car moves off as he crosses the lane and approaches the house.*)

Exterior. He takes the path to the front door. Knocks. Waits. Knocks again. Cut to:

Exterior. He rounds the house by a side path. Stops as he reaches the rear. Stares at something down the garden.
The OLD MAN, *cowled in a plaid travelling rug, sits in a wicker chair, half-way down the thin slip of lawn, working at an easeled canvas.* DRITTEMANN *approaches, tense, soundless. Stops some feet away. Stares at the back of the* MAN's *head; at the canvas beyond, a gross close-up of a woman's face, abstracted from several photo prints pinned to the frame.*
DRITTEMANN: (*In German*) Comrade Drittemann? Excuse me . . .
>(*The* MAN *stops painting, carefully wipes the brush and places it on the easel ledge, his back still to* DRITTEMANN.)
MAN: (*In good but not* echt *English*) My name is James Dryden. What do you want with me?
>(DRITTEMANN *moves slowly forward, lays the shopping bag on the garden table by* DRYDEN's *arm, looks at him.* DRYDEN *sits stock still, not looking. He's the man in the photographs, but shrunken, the life gone, the eyes random.* DRITTEMANN *removes the oilskin package from the Sainsbury's bag.*)
DRITTEMANN: (*In German*) These are yours, I believe . . .
>(DRYDEN *turns, looks at the package for a long time, then at the German stranger in the black leather overcoat, his right hand in the pocket. He takes the oilskin, unwraps it, spills the*

contents on to the table, sifts it with frail hands, scores, letters, memorabilia, a red leather-backed notebook, the passports. Looks again at DRITTEMANN.)
DRYDEN: You speak English?
(DRITTEMANN *nods.*)
Sit, won't you.
(DRITTEMANN *sits in the offered garden chair.* DRYDEN *smiles suddenly, a bleak withering of the lips. The eyes are dead.*)
I prefer English. The cheese was clever. I've been expecting you, I suppose. Most of my life. They say in these parts: the man born to be hanged need not fear drowning. That's

how it has been with me. That's how it is. I count my life in days now, I listen each morning for my last blackbird, not living is no longer a problem, but I will die *here*, nowhere else, it is the only *choice* left to me.
(DRITTEMANN *looks away down the garden, unable to cope, not wanting to hear, realization staining the eyes. Two British Telecom men are at work on a telegraph pole in the next field.*)
(*Out of shot*) So is my wife dead?
(DRITTEMANN *jerks his gaze back to* DRYDEN.)
Or did she finally decide to confess all and go to her grave with a clean party card? It doesn't matter. In a way she had no choice: handing me over would have meant putting herself under suspicion; to save herself and the children . . . she had to save me too. It was something I'd always counted on, even before we were married. Met her in Spain, you know, Rosa, red red Rosa, in the full . . . obscene bloom of her innocence, 'wading through slaughter like Stalin's daughter', I quote myself, an opera . . . I was a child, a child too, nineteen, twenty, seeking the ancient battleground between right and wrong, but I glimpsed what she would never see: the hand of the puppet-master, controlling the dance . . . Why should this interest you? You're a functionary, a thing of the state, in your ridiculous . . . (*He waves a thin hand at him.*) May I go into my house? This is England. Things must be done properly . . .
(DRITTEMANN *stands, white, in dull shock. Long shot of the two negotiating the walk to the house.* DRYDEN *leans on* DRITTEMANN's *arm.*)

Interior. Bungalow. DRITTEMANN *helps his father through the open french window into the small living room.*
DRYDEN: Come with me.
(*He leads* DRITTEMANN *to an adjoining room, even smaller; his den.* DRITTEMANN *stares at the walls, covered with close-up black and white blow-ups of Molesworth women's faces and his cruel painted abstractions.* DRYDEN *waves him to a chair, sits painfully in his own.* DRITTEMANN *sees the unwrapped Gouda on a table.*)

This is what I do now. I don't know why. (*Looks at his thin arthritic hands.*) I've seen these faces all my life: in Hitler's Germany, in Stalin's Spain, in Roosevelt's America, in Ulbricht's Democratic Republic; it's the face of innocence, it's the face of the drinkers of blood. There *is* only power. Those who have it know it. Those who don't must learn it. 'The ones who are ruled carry others; the ones who rule are carried by others.' Meng-Tse, 600 BC. It's the first law of humankind. The innocent think there is a choice. And stop at nothing to prove it. Do you choose to be here, now? You serve your masters. Did I choose to return to my country after the war as an agent of American intelligence? We have both learned the second law of humankind: any life is better than no life. Later still, you learn the third law: it's all one, life is nothing. Will you kill me?

(DRITTEMANN *studies* DRYDEN's *mad eyes.*)

DRITTEMANN: No.

DRYDEN: Somebody will. I expected Americans. They wanted me disposed of years back, I found out, slipped the noose. But you're Stasi, without question, forty years and still the same SS hand-me-downs for uniform . . . (*He laughs, a brittle bark.*) Am I still an opposition hero back there? You have to live in England to learn the true nature of irony . . . But. You know the second law. So you're no fool.

(*A blackbird sets up in a tree outside the window.*
DRITTEMANN *gets up to look out. The men have left the telegraph pole. There's a phone on the windowsill: it has no number.*)

You know what Goethe said on his death-bed? *Mehr Licht.* And you know what? The sun ignored him . . .

DRITTEMANN: (*Sudden*) Was it the Americans who got you out of Holland?

DRYDEN: Holland?

DRITTEMANN: After Spain. Before America. With the Dutch Resistance. In the town of Gouda.

DRYDEN: Gouda.

(DRITTEMANN *turns from the window to look at him.*
DRYDEN *sits quite still, his eyes closed, his mouth moving in the*

silence. Close up of DRITTEMANN. *The echoey voice of the young pioneer rehearses his English structures: 'It is true, it is not true. It is untrue, it is not untrue.'*)
DRITTEMANN: (*Softly*) Did your wife know?
DRYDEN: (*Eyes closed*) Rosa went to Russia. To practise her innocence. To suck on filth. Rosa found her own way to be guilty.
DRITTEMANN: (*Softer*) Rosa fought at Stalingrad. There's a difference.
(*The* OLD MAN *opens his eyes. Stares at him.*)
DRYDEN: Who are you? Why are you here?
(DRITTEMANN *stares at him for some moments, leaves the room. By the front door he catches sight of the white wreckage of his face in the hall mirror.*)
(*Out of shot, from the den*) We pay the price. The last law.
(DRITTEMANN *returns to the den doorway. Watches* DRYDEN's *face from side and rear. Tears seep from the lidded eyes.*)
DRITTEMANN: Schuldig.

Exterior. Lane. Drizzle. DRITTEMANN *heads for town, hands in pockets, shoulders hunched. The Honda appears behind him, skirts the kerb. He walks on.* EMMA *bips the horn. He slows, crosses to her wound-down window.*
DRITTEMANN: (*White*) I need some space . . .
EMMA: What happened . . . ?
DRITTEMANN: He's a mad old man. He's not my father . . .
EMMA: Klaus, listen . . .
DRITTEMANN: No.
(*He backs off from the car, heads on towards the town.* EMMA *watches, tightfaced, hands gripped hard to the wheel. Drives off eventually, passes him.*)

Images of the solitary day:

Interior. City bar, full of students and noontime guzzlers.
DRITTEMANN *drinks Scotch, beer chasers, sombre.*

Interior. DRITTEMANN *wanders around an amusement arcade. Young kids despatch fleets of spaceships to shoot down the aliens; video wars of all sorts are loosed all around him.*

Exterior. Mid-evening. Another pub. He watches a dozen drinkers watch an American war movie on the colour screen above the bar.

Exterior. Night. Rain. Long shot of DRITTEMANN *in a phone box, counting coins on to the box, receiver to ear. We hear the ringing tone over, an operator's voice ask 'Which country?'*
DRITTEMANN: (*Voice over*) German Democratic Republic.
    Berlin. 823706.
    (*He waits. Inserts coins. Waits. Ringing tone. A woman's voice answers in German.*)
    Rosa. Klaus.
    (*Silence. She says nothing.*)
    (*In German*) Rosa, I found my father.

Interior. Menwith Hill Monitoring Station. Three men randomly monitor several dozen ongoing overseas calls, on headphones, frequently switching from one to another, making notes from time to time. In slow track we eavesdrop on several calls – business, personal – until we reach and hold on:
DRITTEMANN: (*Headphone acoustic*) Rosa.
ROSA: (*In German, headphone acoustic*) Klaus, it's not something
    to discuss over the telephone . . .
DRITTEMANN: Rosa.
ROSA: (*In German*) What?
    (*Long pause. The* MONITORING OFFICER's *hand moves to switch. Waits.*)
DRITTEMANN: (*Eventually, in German*) I'm sorry.

Exterior. Night. DRITTEMANN *puts the phone down. Stands for a long time without moving.*

Exterior. Night. He stands outside the boarding house, watching the lit dormer window.
Bring up Casio MT-40, in harpsichord mode, playing 'In Praise of

Nicaragua'.

Interior. Attic room. Night. He stands in the open doorway, watching EMMA *across the dark room. She sits half-lotus fashion on the bed, T-shirt and pants, the Casiotone on her knees. Looks at him eventually. Lifts her fingers from the keys.*
EMMA: Unschuld.
DRITTEMANN: Perhaps it's all we have.
   (*She puts the Casiotone aside. Stares on at him.*)
   You knew.
EMMA: Yes.
   (*He closes the door, scans the débris of their stay around the room. Begins to pack things into bags in a sodden, haphazard way. Gives up. Sits finally on the bed, his face away from her.*)
DRITTEMANN: Everything? Not just . . . Gouda.
EMMA: (*Metallic*) I knew the bones. I knew he did a deal with the Nazis in Madrid. I knew he did their work in Holland. I knew the Americans lifted him in '45, knowing him to be a Nazi collaborator, and sent him back to Berlin a year later. I knew he had been their . . . thing . . . ever since. Also: I knew he was your father. And that fathers are men's necessary fictions.
DRITTEMANN: (*Remote*) I had imagined . . . (*thinks*) . . . we were comrades. Somehow.
   (*She says nothing.*)
   What will you do with him?
EMMA: Speak with him. Flesh out the bones.
DRITTEMANN: Is that all?
EMMA: No.
   (*He looks at her.*)
   I'll try and bring him to justice.
DRITTEMANN: He's old. Mad. Rotted away.
EMMA: So's Europe. We have to begin somewhere. What about you?
   (*He fiddles for a cigarette, not answering. The pack's empty.*
   EMMA *reaches over to a bedside-table, hands him a pack of Marlboro.*)
   Here.

DRITTEMANN: Thanks. (*Lights a cigarette.*) I'll drive you out there tomorrow.
EMMA: All right. You have no reason to trust me.
DRITTEMANN: Don't I?
(*He reaches forward, strokes the fine hair of her head. She watches him steadily.*)
EMMA: Even though I mean you well.
LANDLADY: (*Out of shot, from landing, calling*) Telephone for a Mr Drittemann, is that anyone in there . . . ?
DRITTEMANN: (*Frowning*) Thank you. (*He stands, looks at* EMMA *for a moment, leaves.*)

Interior. Stairway. DRITTEMANN *follows the chuntering* LANDLADY *towards the downstairs living room and the telephone.*
LANDLADY: (*Under breath*) I don't know what the world's coming to, I don't, I was told your name was de Baen, Mr and Mrs de Baen, now it's Mr Drittemann if you please . . .

Interior. Living room. She points to the telephone on the drop-leaf table, returns to the sofa to stare at television, casts a baleful stare at her husband at the other end, who steadily refuses her look. On the screen, Newsnight, *with aerial intelligence pictures of SS-20s being moved into East Germany.*
DRITTEMANN: (*At phone*) Klaus Drittemann.

Interior. Droysenstrasse apartment. LUCY BERNSTEIN *at hallway table, receiver to ear, reflected in a wall mirror.*
LUCY: At last, tracked you down. Do you have a minute, we need to talk?

Interior. Living room. Light from the screen flickers bluely over his face.
DRITTEMANN: Go ahead.
LUCY: The Munich organizers have come back with a bigger offer, another three thousand . . .
DRITTEMANN: What's Munich?
LUCY: Basically it's a pop festival.
DRITTEMANN: Ahunh.

Interior. Menwith Hill. We follow the call on monitors, headphone acoustic.
LUCY: The thing is, it clashes with the Zurich date, which I'll remind you is for travel and accommodation, no fee, no television fee, nothing. I thought I should check again before committing.
DRITTEMANN: Fix Zurich.

Interior. Living room. Close shot of TV screen, between the heads of the watching people. Stunning aerial shots of slow-moving, missile-bearing convoys taken from a hundred miles up.
LUCY: (*Voice over*) Are you sure?
DRITTEMANN: Yes.
LUCY: All right.
    (*Silence.*)

Interior. Menwith Hill. Monitoring. Headphone acoustic.
LUCY: Any luck with your father?
DRITTEMANN: No.
LUCY: I'm sorry. See you in Zurich.
DRITTEMANN: Fine.

Interior. Living room. DRITTEMANN *puts down the receiver, watches Reagan on screen drawing the free world's attention to the threats attendant upon a passive response to this latest evidence of Soviet aggression. Leaves quietly.*

Interior. Droysenstrasse apartment. LUCY BERNSTEIN *stares at herself in the mirror.*

Interior. Attic room, in darkness. DRITTEMANN *stands in the doorway, dimly back-lit.*
EMMA: (*From the bed*) Can you see?
DRITTEMANN: Yes.
    (*He closes the door. Undresses in the dark. Gets naked into the sheets. She turns on her side to watch him. Strokes his face. He lies very still.*)
EMMA: Bad news?

DRITTEMANN: It was the record company. About a concert in Zurich.
EMMA: So what's the problem?
DRITTEMANN: They knew I was here.
(*She takes her hand away from his face, rolls over on to her back.*)
EMMA: You think I told them?
DRITTEMANN: (*Remote*) I don't know. You made a phone call the day we arrived here . . .
EMMA: I called my *mother*. She has to know, it's part of the work we do, and she's been after this man for almost fifteen years. (*Deliberate*) Nobody else. (*Pause*.) Did you ask them? How they found out?
(*He turns on his side, away from her. Silence.*)
DRITTEMANN: (*Distinct*) You should have spoken with him today.
EMMA: What?
DRITTEMANN: Tomorrow might be too late . . .

Exterior. Day. Slow lazy milky black and white windscreen shot of the Dryden bungalow and drive, as the Honda approaches. An ambulance is backed into the driveway, two police cars drawn up outside. Ambulancemen carry a blanketed stretcher from the front door and load it into the back of the ambulance. Six police surround the house.
In the one shot, the Honda stops, reverses into the side lane, drives back the way it has come.

Interior. They drive down the M11, their gear on the back seat, listening to a local radio news bulletin. DRITTEMANN *drives.*
RADIO: The body of a Cambridge man was found hanging from a beam this morning by his fourteen-year-old daughter.

Exterior. The car heads for London. Over:
RADIO: The girl, Anne Dryden, found her father, James Dryden, a retired artist, in the kitchen of their family home on the outskirts of the city. According to Mrs Elizabeth Dryden, his wife, the dead man had been suffering from

depression for some time and foul play is not suspected . . .
Local weather in a moment, stay with us . . .

Interior. Honda. DRITTEMANN's *hand switches off. They drive in sombre silence for some time.*
EMMA: You knew. How?
DRITTEMANN: He told me. I thought it was his craziness.
EMMA: Told you what, he was going to suicide . . . ?
DRITTEMANN: He told me he was going to be 'disposed of' . . .
EMMA: (*After silence*) I don't understand. What's 'disposed of'?
  (*He makes three movements with his hand: pulling a trigger, cutting a throat, tightening a noose.*)
DRITTEMANN: The man had barely strength to lift a glass to his lips. I saw him struggle to stand upright.

Exterior. The car heads on.
DRITTEMANN: (*Voice over*) Perhaps it's an irony he would appreciate, that we led them to him.
EMMA: Who?
DRITTEMANN: What he called 'his masters'.

Exterior. Heathrow departure lounge. They sit there with their hand-baggage, a seat apart, watching the departure board. Amsterdam comes up:
Boarding now. EMMA *gathers her things.*
EMMA: I'd like you to be wrong . . .
DRITTEMANN: It's academic now.
  (*They stand, a bit awkward.*)
  You'll go on with this?
EMMA: Yes, I think so. Somebody should do it. (*Looks at the board.*) If you come to Amsterdam, come and meet my mother.
DRITTEMANN: What's she like?
EMMA: What do you mean?
DRITTEMANN: Is she like you?
EMMA: Me? Not at all. She's serious.
  (*She holds a hand out, he takes the firm handshake. She leaves. He watches her. Over, the routine announcement about*

unattended baggage.)

Exterior. Zurich airport; immigration. DRITTEMANN *waits at the tall counter. A VDU prints out his Western profile. A soldier reads it, impassive, Drittemann's West German passport opened in his hand. The soldier keys on.*

Interior. Taxi from the airport. DRITTEMANN *shares the back seat with* LUCY BERNSTEIN. *He looks straight ahead. She watches him.*

Interior. Hotel bedroom, good, not extravagant, overlooking the lake. DRITTEMANN *sits by a window, composing on the synthesizer and writing it down in a fluent notation.*
LUCY BERNSTEIN *comes out of the bathroom, wet from the shower, swathed in towels. Wanders around the room drying herself. Approaches* DRITTEMANN. *Runs a hand against the metallic headhair.*

LUCY: (*Yawning, fond*) You meet the session men at three, you won't forget? I have to sort some visas out at the Consulate at four, but we could have dinner before the show if you like . . .
(*He plays on, absorbedly. She watches a moment, goes to the bed, continues drying herself. Studies the chaos of sheets, pillows, duvet.*)
(*Across the room, laughing*) You're a bull. You know that? A bull. Twenty years of women's liberation just passes you fellers by . . . Pouf. (*She lies on the bed, swaddled in towels.*) You're fortunate I'm just . . . liberated enough to take it all on . . . (*She laughs.*) I guess you just turn me on, is that a phrase you're familiar with?
(DRITTEMANN *stops playing, crosses the room to stand by the foot of the bed. He's mild, composed.*)
DRITTEMANN: 'Turn you on.' Sure. I've had tapes of every Jim Morrison album since I was at college . . . How did you know I was in Cambridge, England, at that number?
LUCY: What?
DRITTEMANN: It's a simple question.
LUCY: (*Sitting up*) I rang the Dutch girl's editor in Amsterdam.

> She had the number. Simple answer.
>
> DRITTEMANN: Try again.
>
> LUCY: What is this, Klaus?
>
> DRITTEMANN: You didn't need to find out where I was, you always knew. (*American voice*) You're on the A-team, baby. (*He turns as if to walk away. Turns back, grimmer suddenly.*) I shed no tears he's dead. He was a vile, an evil . . . (*stops*) Creature. And what you do to your own is not my concern. But I don't want to be a part of your *pantomime*.
> (*He turns, looks for his jacket, finds it, puts it on.*)
> Serve your master. Just don't tell me about women's liberation . . . (*He heads for the door.*)

Exterior. Montage of the Zurich day: rehearsing with session men; laying equipment; a slow wander across the town, taking in neo-fascist slogans on bridges and standard tourist attractions. In one shot, DRITTEMANN *studies plaques on a tenement wall: two famous exiles lived in adjoining apartments, Büchner and Lenin. Over, the unsung version of the final song.*
In the last beats of the sequence, he approaches the entrance to an underground car park. Reads a sign in German signalling its primary use as a vast underground nuclear shelter for two thousand people.
DRITTEMANN *enters the gigantic tomb. Walks around it. Stands.*

Interior. Dressing room. DRITTEMANN *showers, a slow, concentrated, cleansing ritual.*

Exterior. Open stadium. Dark night. Twenty thousand, mainly young, packed in. Bots, half-way through 'Aufstehen', on the lit stage. The kids sing responses, enjoying themselves. Vast applause. Crowd scan, as loudspeaker announces DRITTEMANN.

Exterior. DRITTEMANN *at piano, in spot. Begins to sing, no introduction: 'Fatherland'. Complex, hard, affirmative: a celebration of necessary innocence. The first half of the song is a modern history of white Europe and its horrors, in the pure German Liedermacher style of early Konstantin Wecker. The song breaks in the middle, lights reveal the band, eight-piece, synthesizers, drums,* horns, Drittemann's piano turns electric, as the second half affirms the necessity of innocence in rock. Fireworks lay out peace symbols across the sky. Long white candles light in ones and dozens and hundreds all round the stadium. Faces gleam at the future from the darkness. Credits roll. The song sinks back to a whisper. We're left with DRITTEMANN *in his spot and the candles. The final lines are spoken, unaccompanied. The spot goes out.*